Echo Blind

Echo Blind;
or Blind to the Gods.
by Adam Collins

May this guide you on your journey

Echo Blind

Chapter One:

"I'm Blind, though I am the last concession in
the world, there is nothing but a cold calm that
comes to me. Darkness, fear and blight are my
closest allies and through necessity, they are my
closest friends. I know them all too well, etched
into my memories so that I understand them
like the back of my hand. They sit behind me,
in front of me and from the shadows their
voices always in case me and around what I
believe is my body, Always the unknown tries
to get in the way of us but as I am tricked into
thinking my closest of allies have left me, I
realise that they are always there because I feel
them all around. From this, I have reached the
greatest conclusion of all. There is no god, not
one, nor many, but mostly not that one of all-
knowing and powerful. For if there was he
would have made me seen the light many years
ago and as my old bones are less mobile, I do
not regret him not showing me the common
sunrise or enjoying a breathtaking day. I have
none of those in my memories or not even in
descriptions. All he has left me is the pain of
thoughts and a women's voice that apparently I
can hear some miles away. Every day I forget
her name and every day she tells me."

Echo Blind

The old blind man stretched his neck out long above his shoulders to allow his muted voice the chance to echo above what he believed to be obstacles all around him but what he could not for sure describe what was actually there. A screech crawled violently out from the back of his gullet, cutting its journey to under his tongue and scrapped past his teeth. "My dear, what is your name again?" His face confronted a number of directions and made a gesture to where his non-existent eyes could be. Moving in quick succession to illustrate his lack of vision and with hands touching the territory around him, he spits out again "Please tell me!" Not a sound could be heard in his distance, only the wind hovered by his ears. With sequence, his hands full of pain slowly raised to an old haggard ear. He grabbed the air around it and shook a lousily clenched fist as if to shake the answer out of his hand. "Mary, Mary was that it? Thank you my dear", the old man bumbled his answer with sweet delight, holding it again in his right hand softly as to not break it, pulling his arthritic grip down his long black shawl and weaving the answer into sacked hole disguised as a pocket. His skin becoming tight irritated his already contentious mood and while pulling his hand from his pocket he left pieces of skin behind.

"As you have told me, that you gave golden hair of curl and lash long and as tempting as I am yet to believe you and are they properly brown and very unimaginative, or golden from a bowl to appears but fake from scholarship, Your gaze I have been told is brighter blue that the marbles created of the most delicate of glass but I believe that they are very grey and blood covered. More lies that come to the misconception of one's fantasies. Felt to be delicate but lungs as black as soil, oily and depraved, leaving many to want to hold you with the itchy fingers. these normal tenancies have. Kindness is filled with empathy and yet I believe I would still find your fingers on my capital, playing with my fortunes."

The old blind man was yet to make any sense with his ravings for he had no fortunes, nor did he have much of anything. A figure to suggest that he had not eaten in a matter of weeks and health that resembled less. Most of his hair had fallen out a what little he had left was long hanging past his shoulders in some cases and tangled in a thin greasy mess in other parts. He had demons on his back. A sore had formed just one of his non-eyes from not washing and less care after the blunt force operation had gone through. The wound had not and would never close. The wrinkles in his face formed trenches of experience to be read like a map on how to bring suffering to oneself and others. Each eye bag hung very low on his face, dropping every day further past his nose and close to his mouth. The last of his teeth stood defiant like his personality, at jagged edges. One had been chipped in such a way that the air brought pain to him but had been for so long that the ache was welcomed like an aged, annoying friend. His mouth had been stained purple from blood convulsed up in the night and showed no signs of being washed away at any time soon. His mouth was framed by a long beard of grey that was thick and more sustainable than the hair that covering the last remains of his skull. The scars around parts of his face traced a journey joining his mouth to his cheeks, which hung slightly from the bones giving a slight mirage that none of his muscle attached his skin to his head. The violent stitching up of his eyelids could not be taken lightly. Punishment for the wild corner preaching and countless public outcries that the old gods were dead, though in his heart he believed that they never existed in the first place. Each stitch was roughly placed across the gap that formed the eyelid and made an incision into the eyeball itself. The old piece of string was now black with dirt and waste, with its colour fading with the fabric as time would, but still held his eyelids together. Each thread had been woven deeply across the eyelid in a broad manner following a cross-stitched path with a small measurement taken to go through the actual eyeball. Thin metal staples that had been hammered into the corners of his sockets held parts of the loose string in place but still, the threads had frayed slightly, this was to continue with the brutality of his punishment. The malice had been thought out enough to continue his suffering for time to continue with even the turn of his head or a wisp of the wind. The pain in his socks echoed deeper into his psyche and was enough to keep him awake at night. Slight cuts had been left on his neck from long sharp fingernails. These instruments of destruction came from his own hands with parts being left in his skin and muscle. His dreams from when his mind finally shut down for short periods of time in the last few days had left him covered in creeping, crawling, monstered marks, large enough as to be noticed and deep enough to be felt in any groove. With this, he had been given the urge to rip these pinheads from all over his being and his physical being did what it could to rip them from his skin. His bones pocked out around his rib cage as his stomach had sunken towards his pelvis and made him seem more tortured than he could have been. His arms, withered and brittle had been elongated with malnourishment and discomfort. His legs covered in sores hid below a cloth that was used to cover what was left of his dignity. The last time any of his being had been washed was when it rained heavily so long ago. He perked up his head for one more shout for what was left inside him for the day.

"Gold has fallen from our souls and now all we have is credit, credit and who is to be paid with that. It doesn't exist for an elderly man like me. No sight, no eyes and all there is will be darkness, fear and blight in my life. Those common friends who have never left me. Spreading fear and uncertainty. Yet try playing chess with them, speaking with them as their words will only contact the death and I even sleep dreams with them."

The old man rested back, his body yearned to unravel but he would not yield to it. His fingers buried into his chest, the pain that had kept him awake at night for long periods of time persisted and would not leave him alone, his head turned pulling on the skin that had been connected to his face. He had been tortured and tormented for the first stages of his life for spouting words that had sounded quite different, most of the unrepeatable rantings that came from his mouth he did not believe, the only truth to these lands, the gods chose their worshippers but non of them, non of the one hundred and seventy-four gods had chosen him to worship them and from that his knowledge had leaned towards the idea that not only was their not one god but there were no gods to begin with. It was a farce created by greedy priests, rapacious bishops, hoggish cardinals and sinful missionaries. Each and every god, the gods of the forest, the giants of the sea, the fortune sirens from the rivers of honey and sugar in the fields of gold. The demon gods of inferno and pedestal gods of misery that hung in the shadows praying on those in the large asylums, with dedicated shrines of human discharge and found items in the hospital gardens. The rapturous gods of chaos that lived on the mountain tops throwing the thunderbolts down towards the unsuspecting sheep, masticating on what was provided and had become a useful distraction for mischief.

The shrine business had never been so profitable. Sellers and hawkers sat, eyed focus on weary travellers to sell them trinkets to appease some god or another. Hoping high for a pilgrim, matching himself to one of the 'Meccas of prayer' said to be the birthplace of whatever god they had. Lucky stones, blessed coins, pieces of bone that may or may have not belonged to a saint or faithful worshipper made famous by a miraculous act of mercy on the world to which change was left in its wake. Yes, even gods had been dedicated to soups and sweet cakes. "Need to charm a lover why not pray to Keta, the goddess of the sweet cakes of the north, she will bless you with the treat that charm the most uninterested of lover." shouted a nearby hawker with a market stall. "three rubs with this before making sweet desserts and then say the prayer with it held over the finished creation will spell happiness in your future." The old man placed his elbows on the floor and gasped for air, he no longer had the strength to carry on his tirade to the world. It had fallen on deaf ears as the locals and feigners alike had ignored him, heading for the local charm sellers. The knife dedicated to the god of the hunt, or some other pastors had gathered the attention of the crowds, as the dust was being kicked up into a frenzy over one item held by one seller, his mouth opened and his musical observe reached up through his throat and spilt out onto the faces of many, anxious soon to be customers. "Quiet all of you" he bellowed into the crowd, "I have in this hand of mine, this right hand a genuine finger of the pilgrim, Saint Jerome of Thanage. He walked barefoot to the sacred site where Chytia, the god of wine and good times had laid the divine holy vines that make the greatest tasting wine. He sipped from the cup made, (they say) of the bark of the tree that produces the golden fruit he took back with him to brew the Cidre that cured an entire village ill-fated and forgotten, cast out citizens. Saint Jerome skipped then over 30 hills where he passed away on the mountain of Yuless, (they say) recreating the wine of the best gods wine possible." The seller was fat to the point his stall, that he was standing on bowed dangerously and creaked sighs of help whenever it could. His beard was ruff and unkept, frail at the edges and dirty. Though it was cleaner than the shirt that he wore, it had grey stains and marks from last nights supper. His trousers had been kept up by two long straps leathered over his great hawked shoulders, which clung to his back in some places and had been stretched by his stomach in others. His commencer trousers had been worn for much time, judging by their state and holes had appeared just above the knees. He had placed between his thumb and first finger what seemed to resemble a bone. It was white, small, had two notches on either side of it and two holes where a string had been fed through it. He moved in a fairly odd style, like a man with a limp due to the fact that the weight of his stomach must have hurt his back and every time he said they say he leaned towards the audience and shielded one side of his mouth from a non-existent eavesdropper. The crowd sounded as to hang on his every word is contrary to the rantings of the old man.

The blind old man harked in his crumpled state, leaning on his elbows. Blood had appeared on his bottom lip in a thick squirm and formed enough for him to spit in a general direction. "Fools," he said to himself "Do they not understand, there are no bones of saints, there was no saint Jerome or any of his ilk, walked over one hundred roads barefooted to find the grapes of a non-existent creation. What rot," he wiped the last of the blood from his mouth and leaned his head on what he thought could be a wall, its ruff texture enlarged the wounds on his head slightly, but with all the pain he was already in the old man took no notice of what more he was putting his already broken body through. With the smallest finger on his right hand, he picked off remnants of what could be dead skin, dirt and vital fluid. His broken fingernails were sharp and jagged for the little protection that could be afforded to an old blind man as he was. "none of it was real" he said silently in his head. He could hear people bidding with their Forins. A king's weight in gold to some, all for what must be some sort of chicken bone. "It could be the real finger of some pilgrim that was just unlucky" the old man let himself think. "… journeying to the temple of luck with any poet licence." The old man slipped and banged his elbow on the dusty ground, feeling pain as more of his head scraped the wall. Instead of yelling out in discomfort he held in his breath, gritted his teeth and spat out, holding to himself the thoughts of the doomed traveller he had made up in his head. "I imagine that he prayed to the luck god of gambling whatever name he or she goes by these days. There is a new one of those months after last month with my memory. Luck to do with cards, luck to do with dice, luck to do with animal fighting, luck to do with people fighting. Luck to do with the weight of the wager. It all means nothing anyway." the old blind man turned himself onto his side in the dusty vestiges of the streets, it helped elevate the pain he was in, head pushed up against the wall. His thoughts turned to the defiant ones, the ones he had when he was tired and in these moods. "Everyone leaves me alone now, I am just an insane blind man, I can't hurt anyone, though it doesn't stop anyone from trying." He wouldn't give anyone the satisfaction of ending his own life and from this he kept on, ranting into the wind, living off scraps he found or was thrown at him, and surviving the occasional beating. All he could do was listen to the echoes in his head as the bidding reached its climax and hope he could sleep. The ever darkness inside his world was no comfort but maybe now he could rest, he thought to himself. The pain had narrowed and the makeshift auction had finally finished with what sounded like a woman, dressed in a long rapped cloth that covered her head, coloured in yellow. His head slid down further as gentle as it could and he slowed his breathing to finally get some rest.

"Sebastian" A golden voice come out of the darkness, "Sebastian," it said, shaking the old man, "Rise, Sebastian rise." The voice sounded heavenly but it disturbed the old man and made his move from his hobbled position but not enough to get up. "Who goes there" he shouted into his ever-living darkness. "How do you know me?" the fear had etched into his voice and with his actions, he put one arm over his head as defence while the other helped him stay semi-upright. "What do you want?" he shouted "I am but an old blind man, I have not any wealth or food for you to consume, please, leave me to rest." the voice issued him with a warmth he had not felt before, it was all around him rather than greeting him from where voices commonly came before he was ridiculed and spat on. "Please," he said, "leave some Forins or some bread and be on your way." wanting to be left in his darkness the old man felt around to make sure he was not being watched over in range and then he sat up. The voice came heavenly to him with a sound of what could be described as godly. The voice came back with a simple enough request to follow. "Sebastian, you must go on a pilgrimage" the voice requested. "Bollocks," he cursed out loud with a reply. "The gods had left me behind long ago, I lost all I held dear to me and then I lost my sight. Taking a pilgrimage will not bring any of it back." he didn't let on that he had stopped believing in the gods long ago and this was the cause of much of his anguish. The voice came back to him quickly and from everywhere, not only could he feel it from inside his head but a cold wind had caught up with his skin keeping what was left of his pelt to stand on edge. "We know!" the voice said, "We know!" it repeated a few times causing some discomfort to an already panicked Sebastian "You have not the faith in us" the voice rebounded off his wounds causing sharp pains, pulling on the stitches in his eye socks, Sebastian yelped slightly and gritted his teeth to subside the pain. "We know," a slight silence followed which lulled into a halt to the pain he felt and let his head recover what thought he had lost a moment before so he could understand what the voice was saying.

"You do not believe Sebastian, you stopped believing a long time ago, you first blamed the gods, all of them for your misfortune and then you started to consider, consider the idea that there were no gods at all. The monks, the priests, the clerics, elders all had built their beliefs on the sand. On and on you went cursing all of them and the people you considered foolish enough to give their life's to the myths and adorations given to spectres of every kind. It led to you lashing out, it led to you consuming, it led to you losing your vision and your sight. Soon you were alone, calling to the winds for coins that many paid you just to give them some quiet. Let us know how you feel? You seem panicked, something you have put your faith in has just been contradicted. There are gods, yes not as some worship, there are many false prophets. These will all be taken care of but we need you. Come to us, Sebastian.

His complexed mind shattered in pain over all of this, the voice was starting to increase the pain in his head and bones. He felt his skin start to itch and with defiance in his soul, he spoke to himself, a few words that brought him strength. "There are no gods," he said quietly to himself. "there are no gods, there are no kings, there are only men and what they do." he had held this theory to him for some time. It was thought many nights, he shouted it many times before his oculars had been forcibly removed from his skull with blunt instruments. "Nothing commands the beasts of the earth, nothing commands the rains or sunshine. Only the fields make the crops grow and the rivers flood when they choose to. Only men are capable of charity. Fortune only favours the bold and cannot be just given to those who believe. Atrocious events only happened out of misfortune and not by some angry divinity that needs attention. No invisible men or women lived in the sky, or in the winds. No monsters walked the earth except those of humankind or animals that were higher in dominion than mankind." The old man turned his head slightly as if to move away from the voice but it was everywhere. No gods lived to pick him for this, "You're all in my mind" he thought to himself silently. Trying to keep his thoughts to himself. "Sebastian" the voice chimed musically. "we are real, we are not just a figment of your last years. We have requested you take this pilgrimage." The voice hurt his head more. Its chanting tones rang in his head, creating more discomfort than salvation to any amount. "This is all a part of my imagination," he thought again "I have finally lost my mind, it has come for me. The force of something in my head, it will rot me for the next few weeks and with any luck, it will take me quietly in my sleep, or while I walk the streets a ringing in my ears will incite and suddenly I will fall forward with my last moments" his thoughts were interrupted by the musical expression he had been hearing. "Sebastian our pilgrimage is truth. You must travel far, interact with those who are in need of relativity in their lives, convince some that their hopes can be achieved while others you will have to acknowledge their own demise." The voice had given Old Sebastian some immense orders on which his old body could be little able to grant. Old Sebastian placed his hand under his chin and thought to himself. "If this voice speaks the truth. No, no it can never be true, it is all a delusion, the end of my life is truly on its way." Old Sebastian straightened his wounded legs. "Prove it," he thought "Prove my destiny is with you. It can't, there is a rational explanation for all of this." The voice chimed up, with heavenly music following it with what sounded like harps, stringed instruments and slight playing wind instruments. "Place your hand to your right, Sebastian. There will be a staff, if you accept our pilgrimage wrap your fingers around the staff and it will lead you to our place on this earth." A slight twang sounded to the right of him. Old Sebastian placed his hand to the ground on his right and ran his fingers up and down what he could feel to be the soft but ruff grains of wood that came from the branch of some tree. The head had been carved with spherical shapes and from what the old man could find from his fingertips small markings ingrained into this long staff. While working his way to the middle of the staff he found some grooves which fit his fingers perfectly. He placed his fingers around and suddenly was given the strength with the unexplained will to rise to his feet. Old Sebastian stood in perversion with a new figure in his body and finding he could breath better, I felt a new light shine on his eyelids for just a moment as the music from the so-called gods went away and then again he was back in darkness. He could hear that the hawkers had been packing their market stalls while he was conversing with the voice. "Maybe one of them dropped this next to me?" The roads had become clear in front of him. "Who could it have been?" Then a slight building of force appeared in his right hand, the staff started to pull him forward and then right ways towards the main street. The staff was now pulling him towards the main gates of the city. This was amusing to the old one. It jolted him pulling like an unseen child towards something it found fascinating. The staff tugged and tapped its end on the ground over and over making a loud strike as it hit the cobbles below. The old man was confused by all this but quickly got his thoughts together. He tried turning to the left, all his body went but his right arm which still followed the way of the staff and with a tense pain shot up old Sebastian's branch. The staff started to prove it was the stronger of the two, Sebastian wrenched his body towards the opposite direction to what he had already begun but to no avail. The staff was winning the small tug of war, and he slowly gave in, started in the direction as to what the staff had started in. With only a few cogent moves from his new wooden friend, Sebastian accepted his fate and was moved down the street, past the main gate paralleled by guards seeing a strange old man being pulled towards destiny and past the main walls of the city he was.

Chapter Two:

The wooden staff still made its way on hot dirt that
had surrounded the city as well as the stone flooring
that had been layered down over one hundred years
ago or so the tale was told. Old Sebastian had heard
them many times before and had also repeated the
legends to the best of his knowledge. He thought of
them again and again but after the moment to which
his eyes had been removed violently from his skull he
stopped, he had stopped thinking about all the tales of
the gods, the old heroes that had come before, the
ones who had done battle with the behemoths of the
plains and righted the wrongs made by the despots
who ruled the surrounding areas. The mystics that had
made deals with dragons and the giants of the
mountains to carve out the surroundings of the city
and to protect it from other beasts, untouchable by
human hands. He knew all of the myths, he could
remember them all off by heart but now the pages of
his mind that these tales had been marked on were
torn, frail and bits had been missing. He no longer
recalled or cared about the creation of Iulla, the
Goddess of Poetry or Moaldir, the God of Spring.
Their myths fell by as did the Legends of Florgic the
Valiant or Samael the Reckless. It all started from the
beginnings of an era and while some of these tales
had been made into statues, jewellery, temples and

religious artefacts, to old Sebastian they had been forgotten to his world. "Who was the first?" he started to think as the staff pulled him along the dirt tracts to his unknown destination. "Ximis, The Goddess of the Beginning." The heat could be felt on his forehead while the ruff dirt could be felt in between his toes. The hot wind rushed past him, moving his cloak as much behind him as it could but his new wooden friend kept them in the direction they needed to face. He felt the sand in the air come in contact with his face, and the more he walked his bare feet built up a soul of dust and sand. Still, with everything continuing around him, he was recapturing the old story told to him by his mother long ago about the myth of Ximis, The Goddess of the Beginning.

"Long ago, there was the nothingness and it only had nihility inside of it. The black emptiness would not let anything around it grow or brighten its surrounding until she appeared. The goddess, as soon as she woke up all was created around her. With the first tear from her eye, the seas had been created, from the first spark of her eye the sun shined, from the first sigh of her breath the nine winds had been created and from a turn of her flesh the ground beneath our feet was soon created. With a broken fingernail, she snapped from her left hand. She then broke the large spear-like tentacles into fragments and plunged them into the soil, placing them in the north, south and east to protect our lands from four of the nine winds. After the mountains had been made she then took strands of her hair, her luxurious flowing hair and placed them around her new paradise, those wove their way into the lands and became the wild forests. Thirsty she laid her hands next to the shore and on taking a sip from the sea she threw her head back creating the sand that formed around the area as it fell from her skin. The salt from her tears was too bitter and after much ponder she used spat at the great mountain of the north and formed what would become The Great River, and there she drank. Refreshed she laid her head down and viewed the sky, watching the blankness above. The sun had started to whine with its power in need of wood to keep the fires going, the heat burning and for the power the sun to move. Ximis created the first of the gods from a dream and pulled Navoha out of her Imagination, Navoha tended the ferocity of the sun but could only work so hard before he tired and so needed fuel to feed the fires that shed light on the crops so they grow, that throws heat on the lands so we do not die. That is why his followers offer wood to his temples so he never runs out."

Sebastian remembered these words from his mother, wiping his face, making sure his cheeks stayed soft as every well looked after child should have. His mother would record the story most times by candlelight on the young mind of the now godless unsighted beggar, Back then he recalled her brown light hair flowed in the winds that lifted as such to the heavens when she walked, her movement made a dance that encouraged the local women to be jealous of her. Her voice could turn most stories into a kind of lullaby that would send Sebastian in his youth to sleep. She always told the long tales of the gods, she wore the markings, read the scriptures, worshipped at the temples and offered to the gods, and in his youth, she quoted the tales again and again, until Sebastian learned all of them off by heart.

"Navoha would tend the ferocity of the sun, moving it across the sky with the power of his moment, but when he would grow tired he would fall to rest, and once he stopped the sun would fall beyond the mountains not to be seen until the next day when he would wake and start again. While he worked he could see Ximis tending to the gardens, Creating the gods to tend the lands, to tend the seas and those to stop the mountains from falling into the seas. In her wisdom, she did not count on the jealousy that spired out of the love Navoha had for his creator. He wanted to be her lover forever, and his rage grew for the other gods. He one day sent a large stone surrounded by fire at Ximis and in a fit of rage ravaged her body in flame. This harmed our goddess of creation, and her body was burned to the colour of ash, but this did not destroy our goddess. Ximis but instead she cast herself into the sky, leaving behind drops of ash that would grow into gods, animals and us, the first men and women who walked the earth to worship the gods. Her biggest essence left the moon and she scattered herself to make the stars. At night when Navoha would rest, she would peer down on us all, loving her creations from afar."

Sebastian remembered from his past looking up at the stars, held in his mother's arms imagining how big the creation goddess could be. He slowed down and his new wooden friend aloud his dragging of his own feet. While the Journey had only just started he felt that the pilgrimage would last more than the end of this day. He may remember the stars he gazed upon once with his mother. He might be gazed on by the star his mother was sent to all those years ago. It was his fifteenth year when his mother had been selected by the High Maianha to carry the sacred bowl of ash. A ceremony that was acted every ten years, an offering of ash was to be made to the stars and the moon. The symbol of gratitude towards the creator of the world Ximis was never attended by the children of the cities it took place, and only could be viewed by those who lined the streets near the temple. Herbs had been collected that found their way to medicinal purpose, stems from local plants gathered in the forests covered in what the divine creator was praised for since the first of us had heard her name. Flowers stemmed from the local rivers which had petals so large they hung towards the ground and covered in the romantic colours of natural brilliance. Pure reds sitting with fiery oranges, mixed with fading pinks held in the sky by deep green stems delicate in the environment and plucked by human hands. The smell of the herbs would fill the air as the offerings had to be mixed in a bowl and crushed together releasing the full odour that would hold all those crushing to a standstill in one moment and bring on visions of full feeling making those breathing close by come weak at the knees and swing with their arms to their sides. After gathering the herbs of the forest and the plants of the fields, one of the main coveted plants was to be gathered on mass and placed in the large wreaths held to those who showed that their faith was unshakable. A plant that was worn by many at the ceremony and used as a miracle cure to most illnesses at a certain type of season.

The plant most prised was the Empurpled Sedra, A plant with five petals that stretched out to receive the sun, a golden stamen that filled rich with pollen every summertime, and on the time of love was warn by every maiden in the land no matter to whom they worshipped. It was strong like the goddess, it was distinguished too. It grew by the banks of the rivers that flowed from the mountains, Purple petals covered in white dots placed as the tears of ash that fell from the cheeks of the deity that the people of this town dedicated so much of their love towards. It would stand tall and proud on the days where the sun was at its brightest and would only bloom after nightfall. The crowds of the city celebrated the first festivals, The old man remembered sitting after the sun set with his mother watching with many neighbours, waiting in anticipation for the first Empurpled Sedra to open wide to the people and show its full beauty. Many would perch themselves near the wild plant they predicted to make it open its worldly secrets to them and signal the coming of the feast and social affair that could erupt into fanfare, while tables would be decked outside with food, great meats hunted from the days, stripped from great beasts, delivered from The Goddess of the Beginning, Ximis. Barrels would be kept nearby filled with large counties of meed, wine and spirit. Whatever the people could gather to spark the jubilation and merriment in their local friends and dwellers of the land. Many lovers had been spawned from the festival. While dancing and recreation of old stories filled the air with fire, laughter and gentle jeer. The younger members of the town would cross each other, touching hand and hand for only seconds, gracing skin with skin while gazing into the eyes of each other. Some would slip away from prying eyes into the nearby forests or the tall grass of the fields. One such festival Sebastian could remember in this youth that with the moon the highest it had been in age, with the stars lighting the sky a pale blue, and the moon shining white light onto the nearby rivers, causing the illusion that it had been turned to glass and the nearby fires to continue the celebrations further to past many hours burst into a crackling of fireflies to such an effect that drunks laughed to high notes at the event they were fortunate to view. That night that had been held in high spirits Sebastian could remember howling coming from the fields and the woods but not of a wolf or dog creature that normally graced the outer lands of the territorial outside but those calls were the vocalizations of young men and women kindling life's together with bonds not to be broken. His father to the knowledge of Sebastian had never seen these celebrations surrounded by Sebastian and his mother, instead, he was not spoken of but instead changed whenever a question of his character ever rose to the stature that needed to be talked about. Ximis The Goddess of Beginning was not to be blamed for this, reasoned with, nor bribed. She could not offer him that salvation, nor the other gods, with no matter of sacrifice, offering, celebration, praise, or good deeds he was destined not to know. Sebastian had not been affected by this, he was curious, yes but through years of not getting the answers from his mother and not learning much from talking to the elders of the temple priests, he continued through life learning what he could, helping the temples and living well while keeping his mother delighted with continued servitude and safekeeping. Up until the age of fifteen, Sebastian had always lived by the guarded ways of his mother, growing up to respect those she came in contact with, leading first in the traditions of the beginner's faith and taking part in most of the ideals that came with a smiling response of she that birthed him.

It came to that moment of his fifteenth year that the High Maianha of the temple and older priest who had grown fat as the years had become many named Elighja. Elighja stood at a height that placed his head comfortably below a door frame but his stomach was wide enough to make that task still trouble, while others had no hope of getting around him. His hood was used not as it should have to keep the main of the temple modest but to cover his white head with large patches thinning as toughs of his hair fell out. His vanity could be seen as he was the only Maianha who would shave his face in certain parts because other parts would not grow and instead left thumbprint like spaces that had made some talk about him. Elighja drank, scoffed the local slices of sugar bread, and could always be seen leering at the young in full distrust, claiming no one outside the temples could be as devout as he was. This was never spoken out loud of course but could be read in his expressions that would fall on his face like leaves falling from a tree. One wrinkle would move first, then another and after that, his full-face would change into an unamused strike filled with fury. His mind was never consulted by the village elders and to some, it was believed that without the temple he would have no power to convince at all. He once took it upon himself to visit Sebastian, more probably his mother with the message that she, that year was to carry the sacred bowl of ash to the temple and lay it in front of the statue of the goddess as the ten-year tradition dictated. Elighja's motives were far from those directed to the beliefs of the Goddess. He for years had followed the flesh of Sebastian's mother and while being swatted at all turns had thought up this gesture to guide her towards his bed-chamber or even to the grounds of the temple if his erotic fantasies were to be consulted. Sebastian was suspicious of the old priest, He looked from the window of their house and gazed at a few occasions where the priest would be slumped in his purple robes while his large stomach would hang over the rope used to tie it together. He drank from large tankers and was remembered to having a full wedge of sugar bread in his hand while wiping away the remains that stuck around on his face. Gold coins had been pressed into his hands on his walks through town, these coins to gather faith never seemed to find their ways to the temple but always into the personal coffers of the

High Maianha. He had got to his position and no one could really end the reality of his buffoonish sermons but he did convince Sebastian's mother to carry the bowl of ash to the temple that night.

In the afternoon she had bathed productively in the river, making sure her skin, and soul was clean and after the sun had set purple robes that had been left in the house by the repulsive priest was draped on her skin with nothing to be worn underneath. The people of the town had lined the streets with torches in hand ready for the ceremony, one by one faces waiting eagerly to see who was chosen for the tradition turned from curiosity to concern and then to anger. Whispers went among the crowd as the white skin of their fellow towns persons arm's lifted a large brown clay bowl, filled with the herbs and flowers ready to be burned in front of their goddess. "She doesn't deserve the honour" one said, "Ignorant strumpet," another said. "She had seduced her way," said another grabbing a stone from the ground and gripping it firmly in her hand. A loud crack was heard in the darkness, a stone had been thrown harshly through the touch lit streets leading to the temple, and in a matter of quick moments connected with the head of his mother, Sebastian watched as a line of blood ran down her face, staining part of her hand with red as she tried to recover for the quick violent at that stalled her. To her, the bowl was all-important and not her well being. She stopped only a second, then continued to her destination with her head held high but with still a small stream of blood etching down her face. Another stone came, and another, these flew past her, but another stone cracked her cheek so violently she fell to the ground. Making sure the bowl was safe she laid there, motionless. Sebastian went running to his mother but found his legs unable to move. Fear wore him like a cloak and now his joints froze with the clenches of unseen stumps making his knees hold-fast. He was in an invisible river of fear that could only watch as the crowd turned ravenous over his mother. One woman grabbed the bowl from her still hands, and walked it to the temple, while others over to the boy that now cluttered their streets and proceeded to let out kicks of fury and pestilence. Some threw stones directly at her stretched out body, while others fell down stops of heavy feet covered in leather and iron. She moved and let out calls of pain for moments only but they fell silent as her body became lifeless. After more fierce shouting, spitting and violence, a touch was placed on her robe as her body was set alight. Sebastian watched as his world fell from the heavens around him, his eyes filled with tears and he became full of motion, his cries could be heard by some of the crowd and a few large men, filled turned their gazes towards him filled with the hatred, wrath and malice that was not satisfied by the brutal execution of his mother. Sebastian turned and ran as fast as he could now the spirits of terror surrounded him. He felt his muscles burn with pain, fill with the acid of power as he fell, full sprinted out of the town and towards the forests. His face was cut but the branches protruding from the trees, his legs had been slashed by the thorns from the bushes and he had been bruised by the uneven mounds that he fell into in the harsh wilderness. His mind would not think of this but instead envisioned the jealously of the women of the village as his mother walked the streets head held high, directed to her faith. She had caused no pain to anyone, lived modestly, helped the temple on the occasion needed and when not asked by anyone. She raised him with no malice and had kept him in comfort to what she could afford from a young age. He would never see her eyes again, not in his memory or his dreams but instead would only remember the look of pure aggression of the faces of those who he once called kinsfolk.

Sebastian remembered that night well, he ran for what to him seemed a lifetime, once he stopped and was convinced that all of the towns-kin had given up their search for him. He fell into a trench and covered himself in moss, that night dirty, bleeding, and with eyes full of tears he fell asleep out of exhaustion from the pain. With these memories flashing in his mind, Sebastian tightened his grip on his now familial wooden friend that was still dragging him, now through marshland. The staff had continued to make the journey with Sebastian still attached as the crow would have flown and now Sebastian could feel his feet sink into the ground. The smell was rancid and cinched the nostrils of all who could be close, which for an old blind man, seemed to be tortured in nature. Sebastian cursed out loud. "Could you have not chosen to go round this infernal smell, it vexes me". His pain could be heard all around him as the ever missed engulfed them more and more, but the staff never yielded, it continued to make its journey with no amount of terrain conveying its slender wooden frame. Sebastian made an effort to turn the other way, but his new friend used its full force to keep going. Sebastian pulled with as much might as his weak frame could allow but the staff kept going and pulled him further into the marsh. His misery from his memory and the feeling of marsh freezing his toes while suffering from the dark world he had been plunged into by cruel hands mounted upon him, tired from walking, dragging his wounded body and thinking of that night which led to the savage violation of his mother had brought him to the edge of his anger. In his dark thoughts he wished a plague upon the new gods he was now in service to. Being pulled faster and faster, gathering in speed, he felt the reeds whip his ankles like that night so many years ago. Suddenly he fell, and the staff stopped while his shell impacted the ground below, he writhed clutching his ribs, with his legs spreading into the mud and his mouth full of water that came from the marsh. His wounds that sat on his face became wet and began to hurt his face more. He razed himself from the mire, slowly not making a sound, hand still clutched to the staff. His mouth hung wide open, coursed in defeat letting all the strength from his fall drain from his mouth until he heard in the distance what sounded to be a young woman crying. Her sobs echoed through the fog that clung to his body, making no direction know from where they originated. He moved his head to get a better sense of where they came from but was still confused as they moved wildly in his darkness. The staff that had remained motionless during his fall started to pull him again, once his balance had been restored. Sebastian was pulled forth until he could feel that the reeds had parted and suddenly he was on the edge of what was to him a lake. The crying had come very intensely on his way, closer and closer but once the staff had stopped he called out loud, "Do you wish for me to continue forward? it is impossible?" He stretched his left arm out in front of him and swayed outwards until he came across a shoulder to his left, after a few moments of silence, he felt tears on his arm and the sobs began again.

<u>Chapter Three:</u>

The young lady's tears felt cold on his osseous forearm. The young lady with fair hair looked down at the old man clutching his staff in one hand and felt his bony fingers on her shoulder. Her tears still descending down her cheeks, stopped for a second as she did not expect another soul to be this far into the marshlands. She held her breath for a few seconds accessing the situation. She could see that the old man was in fewer amounts to having the correct number of eyes. He moved his head in an attempt to catch a sound to know the situation but was greeted with the cold silence of a held breath. He kept his face with no answer not knowing if he was welcomed to the place he stood or if she noticed his eyes would run in horror towards a way that would be most dangerous. After a few seconds, more of the world is left to its own actions, the tears started again and the young lady let out yelps of pain from the deepest parts of her soul. Her pain louder than most of the common animals in the area seemed to shake the earth and continue to encourage birds to take flight from the surrounding tries. Her whales echoed into the heavens but no gods would respond to her sadness and from that, the only salvation she was granted was in the wake of this old man. Sebastian took the full weight of the girl as her emotion overtook her and her head fell to his body. Her tears built up enough to soak his cloak through and supply a river to flood around the pocked bulges in his skin made by protruding parts of his spine and rib cage. She sobbed her worth into him letting him support her frail collection of pains and woes with what little form he had that had been taken on the grand pilgrimage already. He stared at her with non-eyed stitches, hoping that she would collect herself soon but also to try and understand what act? What accident? What insurgent had fouled her for this to be cradled by this much heartache and torment? Finally, once her sadness had been preserved to subside a little Sebastian straightened himself up the best he could and sympathetically raised his voice. "What has happened, my dear?" he asked using his only free hand to calm the girl but stroking her hair and holding her here with part of his elbow to create the illusion she was safe with him. Truth be told if they had been attacked by the wolves in the area, he could only provide a detraction to them and let them tear his fresh apart while she was able to get away but this was not necessary to be thought of at this time. She held him close breathing in as hard as she could, clutching for the words she needed and the strength to stop crying. "He is gone," she said between breaths pulling her head just away to establish a space as not to breathe in his robe. "Who?" Sebastian questioned quickly. "Who? What of this crying, Please my dear please tell me." The kindness flowed from his breath and his long fingers followed their way down the long flowing grooves of her hair, calming as he went, and then repeated to continue the work they were creating for themselves. staff in his hand he seemed like a wise individual and from past experience he had been but with the few years, he had been stricken with a madness that had no cure and had left him to adopt the decisions that lead to him being savagely blinded and left in the streets to die. "My dear?" He asked with kindness weaved into his voice, "What is your name?" the young girl pulled away slightly, whipped her face with her arm and replied with a sweet voice, laid on the meadows that populated lands once used to make beer. "Marellda" a name that helped to etch into the mind of the old man, a young girl with long hair, blue eyes, rosy lips and a small nose walking the fields picking flowers as the young girls used to do in his former village. Old Sebastian had likened her to have lost a trinket, or charm that meant a lot to her, something that may have been given to her at birth, or by someone, she had been linked to so closely that being without them was like a bee sting to the soul, but with all insect bites and stings, it would heal in time. Some things were like that, one day they mean the world only to one person. Entire realities have gone within a blink of an eye as the most important of matter sour and fade to the world. Then as time getting longer and longer and further away from the initial factor the wounds heal and all one day will be forgotten. This was now only a hope for the old blind man, an careless wish to solve a problem quickly so he could continue with his quest, but the world like the gods, fictitious or otherwise was cruel and filled with misfortunes and will take any creature to the brink of madness and direct them to the pathway that leads to the afterlife, or in old Sebastian's case, nothing.

She raised her voice again after wiping away more tears from her cheeks that had been made red with all the sadness flowing through her. "He was supposed to be with me forever, yet he left me with a hole in my heart, I cannot live without him. He was supposed to protect me, look after me, see me and I see him, through the storms, the summers, through all the seasons. We were supposed to harvest the" her cries muffled out and her through made a choking sound, gargling a mixture of sadness, pain and what had happened in her life. She barked out the words "In the meadow". Old Sebastian listened to every word and still tried to keep her calm. He was now her confidant, his quest had to wait for she was in grave distress and she was in need of consoling. Old Sebastian straightened the girl up to help her breath better, and with all the kindness and compassion that a father could give a daughter in need of just the ability to listen. He lowered his head to place his better ear towards her so he could listen to every word she would utter from the red lips he imagined in his head.

She took a breath, holding it for a few seconds to fight her bodies response to fall slumped to the ground and once again become the uncontrollable dismay that she had been before, and then began to relive her tragedy.

"I loved him from the first vision I had of him, standing in the field that day, he was strong, well built, his arms could hold the bales hay above his head with no help from the other farmers. He stood in the sunlight and it shined off his boy making him seem twice as tall then he was but he still was a towering structure of any man that could be described. I dreamed about him the night before, and when I saw him, I knew we were meant to be, forever to each other. I would cook for him after a hard day in the fields and he would come home for a meal, and to be with the children as I mended his shirts. I would not need to be afraid and we would lay in each other's arms from now and until we grew old together. Love will show us the world. It took me a week to gather the confidence to speak with him. I said hello as he bathed in the river, washing the day's sweat from his body, I filled a bucket with water. He in his trousers and boots, leaving his shirt on the bank. I asked him did he need his shirt washed and mended and he agreed, so with a smile that took in all the beauty of the gods. We walked together every day after that, he would talk with me and I would hang on to his every word. I am such a stupid girl, I could not make sense of a lot of things he said. We would take walks through the fields on days we had finished our choirs and we once brought some apples to the fields and ate them under the brandy trees, that was where I kissed him, We talked and talked but I could not contain my love and I brought him close to me, with one hand on his chest I kept him close with my lips and he with mine. We made love under that tree for the very first time and I had the joy as he was mine, forever he would be mine. We met again and again unable to contain ourselves and to be apart from one another, it fuelled our desires to be together again. The days passed and I would wonder when would be the day he would ask me to marry him, I dreamed of that day, He would be wearing his best closes, we would walk to the tree we first was each other, he would get down to one knee, his eyes would light up, I would cry with happiness and he would ask, he would ask me. Elisa, you have made me the happiest man in the world and you are my complete other. You will be the mother to our children and I will care for you from now on. Elisa, would you marry me? I would smile and say yes with all the joy in the world and it would be an autumn wedding, perfect."

She wiped her eyes again, holding on to Sebastian for strength the old man listened to her every word for he had no choice in this matter. It was just them and him.

He stood, cold in his cloak, tired, waiting, listening. The staff had led him to the voice of a young girl in distress. What could an old man such as Sebastian do? The thought had come across his mind that the staff had led him to this young girl and she was part of his pilgrimage, the new gods wanted him to experience all of this episode but for what reasons. How could he consul a young girl on matters of the heart, if she loves this young man why does she not tell him as such. Matters of the heart could be simple like that. Stopping in the middle of blood rushing to ask what was to be happening, that could be the simple answer to a maddening expedition. Maybe they needed his help but what could he do. Old Sebastian felt his knees weak, he had not eaten much since the start of the journey and with his head falling she started a sentence that then alerted to his attestation.

"Soon I found myself swollen with his child, the days would pass and I knew life was beginning inside my own body, I couldn't say no to his desires no now that we had a child coming along. So I told him, I told him we were expecting our firstborn, something that would hold us together forever. The joy of both our lives as well as each other. The joy in my eyes when I told him, I held his hand, brought him to close that he was going to be a father and that we should be married before I give birth, that he, we should get a home together and we would be together forever. He struck me, his hand came straight across my face. His attempt to stop me speaking left a sharp, red mark across my cheek and the bruising would rise a few days later. He looked upon my person not with joy as I thought he would, but with fury, anger, rage. His eyes, I had never seen such malice in anyone's eyes like that on that day. His body reared back like an angry world. Rigged, veins bulging in his body. His hands which held his full strength did not move with the pure rage in his heart. He said horrible things that day, things I never knew he could even utter. Hateful words that the demons could only teach others. He shouted words such as whore, he said how could I have done this to him. I was to blame for this mistake, mistake, he called our child a mistake. He said I cursed him and that I was lying, that it had to be someone else's and I was with other men. He turned and said he never wanted to see me again. He walked away from me, I tried to reach him but he was too fast, I tried to hold him back but his great arms threw me away. I tried running after him but I fell in the fields and couldn't get up. I lied there, filled with the pain I could not understand. Why had he done this to me? Didn't he love me? He held me and I let him feel my love. He only destroyed me and left me in the weeds."

Old Sebastian listened to her words, he felt her anger in what she said and realised the young woman was clutching onto his rags, her fingers buried into the cloth making small holes in his last remaining garb, Pulling at him as her pain was becoming more evident to the blind man. He felt something, something solid, it tapped, banged against his arm, it bruised his thing skin draped over pointed bones. He felt it repeatedly hit him, on his left arm. It was starting to leave more marks on him, used slightly as a weapon against this undeserving stranger, the girl didn't notice the violence she was inflicting on this solemn individual. She had built up her emotions so much that she ran out of breath, heaving from her story she stopped to catch her gasp while the object fell laying on Old Sebastian's arm. The pain continued but now was bearable, the moment had been tense but was a stay in the storm of her breath. he felt this was the time to ask. "what is that you have?, What do you have in your hand?" she moved but he placed his hand quickly over hers, holding it in place, his last show of strength for the day. She couldn't pull her hand away but she spoke again, drawing the breath back into her chest again.

"I faced my parents, told them off what had happened, told them his name, and they cast me out, stupid girl, they scolded at me, stupid girl, putting it about for any man to be, you have brought shame on our home, how will we face out fellow villagers. I told them it wasn't my fault, that we could still raise the child. That I would be a good mother. Out my father said. OUT!!." She shouted to the sky as reliving the moment that left her alone in the world.

"It was just me and the child, I survived, I walked the streets in the rain, finding shelter where I could. I lived off what I could, I stole, I begged, I pleaded. Eventually, I was taken in by an innkeeper. The things I had to do to keep a room, to be provided with food. I cleaned, I cooked, I satisfied. I did something no mother should do. Then I couldn't. I was too far along. I couldn't move as far, it hurt. I couldn't. He tried to throw me out. Cast me to the world. The rains would stop. I begged him not to, I felt the pain, the coming, I said I could make it up, I swore to him I would, the pain kept coming and I fell. I had the baby right there in the hallway. A mother shouldn't have done that. Weak and still in a state, he cast me out into the world. Could no longer give him anything he wanted. I had no more gold, and no more favours he wanted. I walked to the alleys where I was discovered. The nuns of Iysus took me in. They cared for me for some time, but even they had limited space and as I got better they too had to tell me to go as well."

Finally, he felt what had been clutched in her right hand, attached to a long strand of string was a medallion, carved into a cherished softwood was the images of a woman with her palm outstretched and an eye in the middle. Her head was decorated with circles meant to be beads and stones of great power. She looked like the women of the lands far away, the tales of female warriors, strong, holding council, wearing amours that showed great monsters they had defeated, made of metals with amazing artisan etching and riding on the backs of horses while defending the honour of there many males they kept to cook and care for the children. These magnificent women had stories of them holding court in their tribes and deciding the direction in which they should go. Mysterious concepts to some of the warriors in the lands, even where Sebastian inhabited. They could come from the taverns, heavily intoxicated, joking on what it would be like to have one of these empresses as a wife, others commanded that they should be subjugated to the wills of man, as such it was written by the gods. These men didn't realise that these combatant mothers, daughters and all sisters in their own principles had their gods. Gods by their descriptions could take on a dozen gods of war or the gods of chaos. These women, hunted, fought, drank, created, fished, warred, debated and loved through time and tales enough that to some of the villages in other lands they had become a myth. To Sebastian, he was never to criticise but only to admire the stories he heard, and now thinking back to the tales told around campfires from land to land that he found himself in, common stories of the gods, commons stories of heroes and common stories of these warrior women. These women worshipped one goddess, one goddess above all. She had icons scattered around the lands, brought forth by the priestess of the warrior clans, tough to villagers who then migrated from place to place, teaching others of her and her deeds. The Goddess of Forgiveness, the goddess Iysus. Prayed to by peoples who had no certainty after death, those whose deeds caused harm, pain, sadness or death. The nuns would set up temples in barns, empty houses and as places of worship went these holy grounds always seemed to be more on the modest or as a found side. Never containing alters but small humble shrines. It was said praying to her would ease one's conscience, but too old Sebastian, he was yet to see any miracles due to the worship of the goddess. The old man placed his other hand around her arm, not to scare or to threaten but to calm the young girl, but this action failed.

"The child wouldn't stop screaming and crying, it is all he did, I tried to feed him, but he rejected me. I tried to care for him but he didn't agree with my care. He kept being warm and hot in the cold weather. I couldn't care for him, I ran dry. No one would take us in. I heard the villagers whisper. They used words like whore, was that what I am, I made the mistake of love. That was my only crime and now I was meant to suffer for it, the stone I was to drag around my neck was made of flesh and bone and assaulted my senses every day. No one cares for a girl whose child is fatherless, the boy was a signal to everyone that I was not fit to be a wife. I had not slept well since the birth and now he was draining my life with his incapable need. I walked with him, for a time, my mind not able to focus, I must have walked for a long time because when I raised my head, I was here. How I got I could not tell but my footsteps would lead me back. The child had stopped crying, I hadn't named him, not properly. What kind of name could I give a burden. A leech on my life. I stared into the water. It looked soothing, he was still so hot and I got into the water up to my waist, it went brown and cloudy as I disturbed it. Like my life, turned the water unseeable and spread to out of view. I let him rest on the water, it seemed not to bother him, he was so hot before that I think it was comforting. The poor little thing, he must have tired himself out. He was so light in my hands then. He didn't weigh a thing, he was not a trouble. I felt the cold air on my cheeks, the water around my legs started to warm up, I was in the middle of nowhere with no one around, the gods sent no words to help me. I fault of him, the one who left me. We were always meant to be together but we had been broken apart by something so small, something that fit in the wells of my arms. I looked over the child, he didn't move a muscle, he reminded me of him. I lowered my arms slowly, deeply into the water and he never moved again. He went cold, never to be warm again. I just stood there in the water, weeds all around me, silence in the air, not one person calling me any names or giving me sharp looks, just blissful silence. I went back to the nuns to ask for some food a few days later. They read me well, asking where the child was, they could see by my muddy clothes where I had been. I was now a sinner, I could become a nun, pray to the goddess of forgiveness. But they wouldn't accept me, mothers leaving their babies in reeded lakes is unforgivable, even to the goddess who forgives all. It appears there are some things even holy women can't cure l. The nuns give me some bread and the medallion and sent me on my way. I was told to pray where I committed the crime. So I did and I have been here ever since waiting, praying to the goddess but I have had nothing in return. Now the water looks so nice, even in the mist it shines, I can't see either of them now, I don't think I ever will."

Old Sebastian, said nothing, his hand had loosened its grip, he just stood there cold. In the mist, he had not been led to someone who needed help but he had been led to a monster. The staff, his new wooden friend had allowed him to release his palm from their steady grip and now he clenched the staff with his right hand tighter than he had done before. If he wanted to say something, his words boiled inside him but yet he remained silent, it was the only thing he could do. He let his head hang towards the muddy ground under his worn and battered toes, barefoot in his position he didn't move a muscle not knowing what to think. Not a tear could form in his forced closed eye sockets and in his position he could not go anywhere, he had no more strength to back away. He found no strength to raise his arms. His only response was silence. She looked at him, her new companion, this old man who had felt pain before. Such violence had been cast on him, worse than what she had experienced. Yet she had not asked him. The old man only stood there, waiting for one hand to fall by his side while the other holds tight his wooden staff. A courteous fellow, but he had listened to her for so long and only interrupted on one account. They both stood there in silence, she held his fingers in place over the medallion, still feeling the grooves of its display. "Why should, did you listen to me?" she asked but the old man stayed silent. A few moments passed where only an odd gust of wind would pass. She breathed, "Do you believe in the gods?" Her question again was greeted by silence. Old Sebastian kept quiet for a few moments, he was angry at this moment but something stopped his words from falling from his spiteful orifice. He had cursed people in the streets around him for much worse actions, for just being alive or for buying religious artefacts in the markets near where he had chosen to spit his words out and yet now he stayed quiet. She slid her palm out of the grip they had once shared leaving the medallion in the scared hand of the old blind man. She stared at him, for a moment while his lips gathered the ability to say a few words without letting his fury take hold. With all the experience in his former vile whit towards those to which he deemed deserving he was only able to utter a few words. "I choose not too" The old man didn't move his head, just while still facing the earth below. "I choose not too" These words, seemed to ring slightly in the young woman's ears. She Starred at him, not moving but instead as still as a butter flight on a petal, only moving to the wind. These words though not vicious or spiteful in any way seemed to inflict more damage than anything else he could say. No one was to forgive her and defiantly not him. He stayed motionless with no sound, not giving her words nor was he giving her any kindness, just standing facing her. She withdrew the bread that had been given to her by the nuns, took his hand and he tried to pull it away from her as to not accept anything from her. She placed it in his hand between his thumb and his two smallest fingers while the medallion still hung from his index and middle fingers. "Here," she said, "you look hungry, you haven't eaten in days". There she was knowing it was the only food he had come in contact with for the last few days and being overcome with his better judgement he held onto the bread rather than throwing it away into the nothingness of his mind. The young girl turned towards the lake and stared into what had been forever and a day. She had not rested, the screams still haunted her, she heard them far in the distance over the water and into the mist. They never left her alone. After some point, a calm had fixed itself on her face and she placed her left foot into the water and lowered the rest of her body, disturbing the waters and muddying the lake once again. She waded slowly towards through the reeds, further into the mist until only her subtle reflection in the water could be noticed. Old Sebastian felt the medallion in his hand, he knew the stories of this goddess well, but could not bring himself to throw away the charm either. Coming back to the world from his self-preservative meditation he slipped the charm using one hand, over the head of the staff and tied it a knot in the thread, tightening it to the long piece of wood. There it hung, swaying from east to west and north to south. The staff moved and the pilgrimage began again and into the mist, he was led to not knowing if he would have to experience more fates that proved to him that if gods truly existed then there should be no more places for them the world.

Echo Blind

Chapter Four:

The staff pounded the mud of the banks of the small lake while dragging the old man behind it. He wished to stop but had not an idea how to control his new friend. His mind had been occupied with his self-concern while meeting the young girl who now had disappeared into the lake. "Why didn't the gods stop her, can't they create everything, couldn't they have saved her, provided her with some kind of a saviour. Stopped her from relying on the Goddess of Forgiveness." Still, he walked deep in thought not taking into account where the staff had been leading him, To him his lack of words, not being able to deal with something like that, she had already comminuted her sins. Nothing he could have done would have changed that, the gods didn't exist, this was just some form of madness. His mind started creating more ideas as to what could be the answer to this brief encounter in his life. "What if the gods do exist?" this concept dishearten him even more, it provided him with some recurring ideas that he had had before which lead him to the theory which came to him a time before the forced pilgrimage. Maybe the gods, if they did exist, just didn't care. They had grown bored with their creations or their duties and now would prefigure to recline on grand thrones and watch our monstrous suffering while gorging on whatever consisted of the height of divine victuals. He placed his only feeding hand holding the bread under his chin, ruffling his beard while being dragged throw lands of uneven lands. The staff had led him away from the nearby waters of the lake surrounded by reeds and towards small mounds that naturally appeared into the distance. The staff guided him to the foot of the hill, and then stopped for a few moments, with enough time for old Sebastian to catch his breath, he placed his foot forward striking a pose to stead himself and felt around where the staff had stopped with his biggest of toes stretched out, arching in a wide range to understand his surroundings. In front of him was now a new challenge for him to overcome. The mound was taller than the houses Sebastian had remembered from the village of his childhood, his new thoughts had sat in his head and realising that the all covering darkness that he lived in had denied him the possibility of seeing anything that had come for him. He was unable to know what the young girl he spoke to looked like or to tell how her suffering was affecting her outward features. His impression since that day his oculars had been removed was that he was never to care about anything his gaze would normally have laid upon. What was the point of looking on beauty if he was made to feel that he was to thank some romantic cognition of deity for it being in front of him? He was not allowed to eat until he thanked the gods for providing and he always had to watch his words or he was to offend someone for worshipping something he did not agree with or believe in. The dogma was to never control the thinking of his mind or the implications of his actions again and with the violent act of his eyes being removed from their rightful place, he then refused to let anyone control his aspects again. He had praised in the past, yes, but now he would sleep without thanking the Goddess of the Beginning, or thanking her for the rise of the sun, he scoffed as some would thank other gods for that remark and how they could use one or more in their prayers. He remembered seeing younger adults wearing the amulets of multiple gods and kissing them all hoping one would hear their prayers. Others believed that their gods were the only ones to exist or better in some ways. Stories of wars thought over different ways the god of fertility had been depicted in sacred texts. "Of course man should be allowed to breed with harems after the thirty-day fast in summer, that's how the replenisher of the fields wanted it." a voice in memory of a debate said. The recollection of the debate sparked in his mind, suddenly candles of light danced in a tavern while forming fortified barriers on a wooden table and sparing a drop or two to slip through the paces provided by slats. "No, man is only allowed one woman and they mate for life, that is why in the marriage sermon between both man and woman they have their hands bound, to show they are now knotted and never to be apart." the second voice, pushed back a tankard of ale to demonstrate he had laid a full stop to his words. Sebastian had realised this memory was one of many debates by like minds, as long as the belief of something about all humankind existed. It was a time before he lost his faith. Many of the justified followers to the gods dedicated towards humanities continued existence tended to be able to debate, question and live peacefully with those who believed in other gods of similar design and origin, as long as the belief in the gods was found inside a working heart, body and soul. Worshippers devoted to the gods of birth, lands, fertility, healing and well being could sit with each other, debate the right ways of worship and continue to sit with each other, while not letting the arguments get over each other's heads and through the temples or practice of worship was different and occasionally bizarre to the others, no ill will was ever aimed at it. "Sebastian" a voice raised, "Surly you agree on the matter?" Sebastian remembered him looking at the other men with silence in his throat, while raising the tankard to his lips, he stopped, a third voice in jest raised above the other two and with a mouth full of meat pie he delivered his insight to the other two. "No point in asking Sebastian" the friend said with a line of gravy marking his chin. "He doesn't believe in the god of fertility, only one higher power for him." The man placed his arm around Sebastian and pulled him close in with enough subtly he spilt only a few drops of his drink on the table. "Friends" Sebastian spoke up, it is not in my opinion on how both of you worship, as long as you adhere to the words of the faith" he answered with diplomatic precision. The other two men looked at their friends and pieced the meat with knives and lowed it into their mouths. The second man spoke again "If we don't ad hear to what has been spoken then we shall go to Tophet, there our loved ones will be set upon by the great beasts that walked the earth long ago, doomed to watch them rip the flesh from our bodies" you are wrong, we will be banished to the lands of drought and there we will have nothing but the sands of the barren to fill our stomachs" both men's ideas came from the different ways the god or gods of fertility had been seen. It was rumoured that just across the sea a tribe said their god was a woman and needed offerings of corn to make sure that the tribes could have sons for generations to come. This was ludicrous to these scholars of their own faith seeing as they had their own answers to how was the right way to worship their gods. Sebastian viewed this as it came, it didn't bother him too much at the time. He was old enough that he had his principles and young enough to explore them. Remembering in his head that by those years he had thrown off the worship of Ximis, The Goddess of the beginning and now worshipped in temples where there was no purple robes or stones to be thrown at him, he had forged a new life at that time. He had friends, he earned what he needed and it was young enough that he had no one else except himself to look after. How times could change in those instances, he found himself thinking of the days they all were filled with joy and saw them all drinking in the dens until the candle went out and the men faded into the darkness of his mind.

Old Sebastian found the staff pulling him again, only slightly but the force was building up. From the position of his foot, he had guessed his next few steps would be steep ones. The mound in front of him was to be climbed and his wooden friend would not allow him to rest any longer, suggesting that slowing down would involve in the most extreme of cases, rolling towards the foot of the raise and starting again from the bottom up. He raised his foot in the air to take a stride forwards, using the wooden staff to pull himself further ahead. After that, another step was taken followed by another until he moved briskly across the mound and up the slopes. He placed the bread he had received in his mouth and took a bite. This would now be used to help him grow, these so-called gods had placed a grave challenge on him. He was to travel great distances at their beacon to hear words, in-person to hear the wisdom of a plan they could have just told him in the place he lay as he starved in the streets. His wounds throbbed as parts of his muscles used high amounts of motion to cut his way across and up. This mound to him was becoming more and more like a hill as his toes dug into the dirt and grass below him. Each step tired him more and with that built his resolve stronger and stronger, this madness that had taken him would not drive him away and if he had to walk towards death to see it through then so be it. He had no more fear left installed in him, he had the wooden staff pulling him towards some goal in angles that he could feel when the staff would guide him towards another direction. He had been shown the start to answers some had been asked and the entire answer he would be given in the end. Never had he shied away so far, and now he would grow higher and higher. Placing the last of the bread into his mouth and ferociously chewing on the crust. He freed up his left hand and grabbed at the ground helping him hoist his old, bony body higher up this natural obstacle. His actions grew in speed, his resolve strengthened to iron. His faith in himself became that needed to scale the now, hill. His sweat ran all over, while his legs gave way every few yards, causing him to fall slightly but digging his now black hands into the soil to stop him from tumbling to the ground. The falls opened up new wounds, he scrapped his hands against sharp rocks and pointed stones, causing the skin to be pulled away from his fingertips and knuckles. His hands made slight spasms and showed pain all the way to his bones. He felt the cold on his back and filled his lungs with the air as he expelled fiery from his chest. His rags left pieces of themselves on parts and while he climbed higher and higher green and brown marks appeared around his knees. The darkness in his sight had stopped him from moving far, he had not left the city since his vision had been taken from him, but nothing was going to stop him now not until he reached the top, only then could he rest. After being forced to crawl further up the hill his hand grabbed what, by touch seemed to be a flatter part than there had been before. Old Sebastian used his last might and pulled himself up, staff in hand and ascended above what had he had wanted more on this day than what he had before on the pilgrimage. There he stood, both feet stable, breathing heavily, sweat running down his face and blood all around his hands from small fountains being pushed by the rate of his heart. He held his breath and listened. Feeling the nipping hands of frost on his face as he fought that distraction and heard what appeared to be the sounds praying close by. The wind blew him forwards, trying to hold himself he leaned back with them everything he had left as to not fall over. There he listened carefully to the words being spoken and evaluated what they meant. "Please, bringer of the farms, bringer of the children, do not punish us further. We have found he who has been spilling great stains on your divine words and has been punished for being barren in our pastures. Please oh great one, hear our pleas and accept offering our offering so our next harvest will support our villages and we can tend the fields in coming years." The spent husk that was Sebastian's body was now starting to bow under his own weight and he felt his legs shaking below him. The prayers had stopped flowing from around the area in front with the words "In his divine recreations we shall tend the gardens." and followed with a few male words together of "amen" and silence for a few moments. Sebastian felt himself falling as his knees gave way to the lightweight that was his malnourished body. Two hands placed themselves under his arms and kept him from meeting the soil below him. "Calm now" a voice paled over him. "You didn't climb up that hill, did you? That's a dangerous one that is," The accent of the voice seemed more burgher than he had been used to in the past and seemed to have the stereotype to belong to someone who tended the fields. His hands were big enough to hold the old man's frail body from collapse and smelled of the earth they obviously maintained. "Durk!" the voice shouted, "We got an olden here, tired, just climbed the hill, badly kept too." Durk closed the holy book he had been reading from and walked towards Old Sebastian and a strong boy who was holding him up as a doll would be. "Keep your voice down Boddy. Have you no respect for the gods, this is a serious matter on account of the harvest. I don't want to be setting fires next season." The older gentleman of the group looked at the boy holding up the old man and decided to investigate further into the matter. "Who is that olden you got there?" the voice spoke while laying sounds in Sebastian's ears like twigs. "I dunno?" Boddy's voice replied softer than he had spoken before, "but, his eyes have been gone, Durk" a loud thwack sounded which was followed by Boddy's yelp. "Shut up Boddy," another voice spoke up. "You never know if he was a punishment, I'm sorry Durk, you know the boy is still young and learning his way in the world." Durk stood watching the old man be held up by the arms. "You stranger, who are yah? Why are you here and what gods do you worship?" Sebastian thought slightly but replied quickly, he knew these burghers meant him no harm if he was not going to be any trouble for them. "My name is Sebastian and I am but an old blind man. I am on a pilgrimage dedicated to me by those above me." "and gods?" Durk asked. "The truth is, I know not their names. They came to me in my lowest of hours and gave me this staff. It led me here. If you do not believe me, throw me down the hill I just climbed or leave me here, I do not want to be any bother to anyone. I have no ills with anyone and wish only to continue when I can." The burghers stood quiet, waiting for Durk to order them what to do. "He has cuts on his head, he looks like he is bleeding and hasn't eaten much in days. Bring him with us and we can get one of the wives to look after him and send him on his way in the morning. Nightfall is soon and he will be eaten by the wolves if he stays out here. Boddy, bring him with us." The group started moving and Sebastian felt himself being carried by this young soul with the strength of an ox. Sebastian felt it inside him, he wanted to know and the question rose from him and was asked to this young one. "Who was the sermon for?" "Terace" the voice replied "Had it all that one did, cottage, four fields, five, beauties to breed with, a seat on the council, he had it all. Well, we gave him three winters. Three winters we gave him and not a sausage. So it had to be punishment then. Having someone like that in the village would have angered Brylan and what he could do hay? Turn our fields to salt, purge our livestock, sour the milk of the goats and run our village barren. We lost a few youngens this year and..." The thwacking sound came again and Boddy moved in pain. "Shut up, you run your mouth too much. "Telling strangers of the village business like that. You will never get chosen to breed if you don't use your smarts." After the disciplinary remarks made towards Boddy, the group went silent as they walked down the other side of the hill. Sebastian knew of what he spoke well. He knew of Brylan, The god of Fertility well and what punishments came to those who could not produce children. Like the tales had been written in his holy texts, failures to reproduce had no right to walk this earth and had to be sent back to the god, so as to be punished forever in the afterlife. The mist started to clear as all the men descended from the hill and as the sun started to set on the horizon, the silhouette of an old oak tree could still be seen. The tree prominent and strong had branches that stretched in all directions with thick bark flaking off in places. It stood tall on its perch with only itself as the company now that the ceremony had ended and all the men had left it to watch the sunset. Tied to the trunk of the tree was a thick rope pulled tied while the other end had been formed into a circle and placed around the neck of the lifeless remains, its eyes looking words the ground while its feet dangled towards the ground. The hanging left its mark against the skyline that could be seen from miles around.

Chapter Five:

Being carried to the village by strong hands gave
Sebastian a few moments to think about the situation
of things. The staff was still placed in his hand but
hanging still in the actions of being handled by a
sleepy child. He knew his days had been lead astray
leading up to the situation he was in now. "Stupid
Burchers," he thought in his mind, he still waited on
the existence of the gods and the practices used to
make them favourable to the personal achievement
and common order of those who worshipped them.
He was once like those whose company he was in
possession of now, but not as extreme and the
absolute being he worshipped never really needed
major sacrifices or inspired hatred of such brutality,
except in the case of his mother. Before the age of
fifteen, he had never seen real impairment. He
wounded through life not witnessing much of the
human condition except daily worship, hardships in
the fields, the coming of age festivals that were held.
His first faith had some strange superstitions looking
back. The invitation of the mothers to newly married
women on how to treat their new spouse was a
strange one. He remembered seeing them all take tea
together in one of the homes and listening to odd
conversions that to him at the time made slight sense.
How to cook and clean home was obvious but then
the taking of him after meals and always make him a

position on his back to help conceive and stranger ideas about bringing those into the temple and laying down the flowers to bring more fruitful tidings. He realised after having to grow that these helped the village create and educate its newer generations. These thoughts helped occupy his mind but it still didn't help that faith was used to justify violence on others. The more mundane gods like the ones for salt, soup, hygiene, cows, metal and lost items just needed some words to be said, offerings of carrots or onions in some cases, washing five times a day on lectors day and grand feasts in springs some time, he had never heard of someone having to have their thumbs hacked off for adding the pepper first before the salt, though he had watched the salt worshippers say their prayers over the mistake, cross their hands to the forehead and down to the knees and back up again as an act of "apologia" for their forgetful natures or not taking notice of their actions. "The stupidity," he thought again while being not being able to do much of anything else. he commented on the density of people's actions once he was told about the hanging man that he was unable to witness being offered to the gods for his mistake. "The men sacrificed him for not breeding in three winters. His women are to be designated out to others. Had anyone bothered to view the situation logically they would be able to view this situation in another light. Did anyone consider the wives? How did they feel about this, being offered to one man and now just being passed onto another in the hopes he is able to produce children. Seems like a waste of humanity to me, boneheaded doctrines." Sebastian had heard of those who worshipped the fertility god Brylan before. He once sat and drank with men who worshipped him in different ways, though the god had only one way of being pleased and that was for children to be produced. The waste of life was only to be used to replenish the soil, while the plants were to replenish the earth. Nothing was to be wasted in most cases. They kept giant heaps in their villages, filled with rotting produce that stank to the paradise fields in the next world or whoever believed in the fields. It was considered an honour in some cases to give yourself to him, but to Sebastian, it was wasteful for a human being to give up everything and offer themselves to an all-powerful something that didn't really exist.

The Legend of Brylan, The God of Fertility was not widely known to most of the people who walked the earth. Sure his devout persons could be distinguished and made their beliefs know through the lands as most can, Those who believed in the Gods of Fertility usually would look towards the worship of his so-called brother, Moaldir, known to most as the God of the Spring, fertility and the new beginning. The Legend that was mostly interpreted that both the gods crawled their way out of the seas and while one was gifted in the art of creation and would take up the reins of bringing back the forests to the full leafy bloom that was needed for the wildernesses to come back to life, Brylan could only bring on the reproduction of the living mammals on the earth. It is written in the holy books kept in the temples of spring that the more powerful god, Moaldir would as always bring the coming of the season, after the great winds would stop bringing the frosts and Moaldir would set about the forests, his body, green and made of the vegetation that he spawned, would run through the lands causing to awaken all that had gone to sleep through the bitter winters. The worshippers to Moaldir would welcome the coming of spring with feasts and weddings. These devote believed according to the stories of the holy text that Brylan grew tired of how the votaries of his brother would engage in the idea that only one man and one woman could produce together and no others after, they believe it he punished some of his worshippers saying that man and woman should produce as many children as possible, any way possible and that just having one man betrothed to one woman would not produce the number of children to please him. The Brothers went to fight over the principles and Brylan was defeated, banished to the sky. The followers of Brylan tend to view a different way the story places out. They could be heard saying that the god of the spring is being ridiculed. In fact, that man should be in servitude of his being rather than being in servitude of the lands. The details escaped old Sebastian in time, but he had remembered stories of the great wars over the strife of which god was the right one and which was the right way to worship him. These times had simmered off after decades of bloodshed and now both sects of devotees tended to get along realising that both worshipped gods that were related.

Old Sebastian had only really heard of two temples dedicated to Brylan, The God of Fertility. The place had a few holy women. These young ladies of maturing age would be considered the most important of all and cared for higher than the reverends. They lived on temple grounds were not permitted to leave while being cared for in the institution of replication. Dressed in a light blue vale of fabric wrapped around parts of the body and keeping them from being completely reviled to the temples grounds, the women were encouraged to take care of themselves and were called the Sirens. Older Sirens could be seen taking care of the children and being good to their promise of Brylan. The Sirens of Brylan were known through the land for being the most fertile of women. The average Siren was rumoured to conceive at least fifteen times in her lifetime, while the temple would take care of the children for a short while. Many of the children had been sold off to villages to be trained as farmers, land cultivators and to refill the villages that had a dwindling population. Mostly Brylan was worshipped by those in small villages and shines would be erected in hopes of keeping their houses from disparaging into the ashes of history. It was normal for the youngest of the children to look after the old and some families reaching up to twelve children but only able to sustain five of them. Villages that belonged to the Burchers tended to run in a fashion that had been developed. Fifteen women would be selected as "breeders" and three or four men would be used as conceivers. In the cases of small villages of thirty to forty people with the constant worry of their faiths disappearing, everyone tended to share responsibility. Women would raise the young, cook and keep the village in order. The men were tasked with producing food, wood, water, shelter and items for sale to other villages to buy that could not be made. The best of these males would be rewarded with the title of conceiver and would be allowed to take wives, But the punishment was grand for not being able to output the generation that would be taking over from the last. Old Sebastian held his thoughts close. The idea that hanging one of their villagers and offering up to God who was mostly in want for there being more people in the world in an attempt to please him was slightly backward. With this, his hanger subsided and hunger instead took over. "Not long now, yah hear" Boddy spoke up, stirring the old man from his thoughts. "You can see those lights, that's the village" The young man obviously had something wrong with him, whether it was his memory, a lack of intelligence or his process of observation was not evident to the old man in this moment of transport but it was, in fact, an unwelcome interruption to his long day. "Can yah see it?" His voice raised again being filled with excitement and was followed by a silence waiting for an answer. The old man replied quietly and as calmly as possible. "I am blind," he said. Boddy moved him down to get a better look at his passenger and starred at the stitched wounds placed on old Sebastian's face. "Oh sorry, I had forgotten about that, It gets me excited when coming back to the village. Tonight Mary had been baking Ferny Pie, it is a sweet delight. My favourite of sweets that be. It will be warm, covered in syrup from the fruit making it sweeter and then it will be washed down with that Parsons ale Durk had been brewing. I ain't had some of that in longer I say." The excitement grew in the boy's voice. He had so much joy that he had not noticed that he was now dragging Sebastian's feet on the ground as they walked. "Can you pull me up, this is hurting my feet a lot?" Sebastian spoke to the young lad and he realised and raised him back to where he once held him.

The men were not greeted by anyone as they entered the village but instead paced their ways through dirt roads to a wall of silence. They neither one of them enjoyed their offering to the god and instead took their duty as one that needed to be wrapped in dignity. The men gathered in the square and said their goodbyes while Sebastian was being held up by Boddy. "Boddy" Durk called the young man, "time to go home, you want to catch a death of cold?" Sebastian felt himself shaking as the young man picked up speed and took him inside a cottage bigger than the others in the village. "Hallo Husban" A voice came forward as Sebastian felt the warmth heating up the inside room. Durk marched up to the woman and brought her close to him for a kiss. Her voice came with a rough approach, while he seemed to relax in contrast to how he had spoken before. Boddy brought Sebastian into the middle-sized room with a strong interior wall made of heavy stone. It supported a fireplace that had been blazing for some time, Sebastian was placed on a chair right in front of the fire and rested the staff on his shoulder while still holding it in his right hand. Durk pulled up another wooden chair and sat down next to him while the women looked at Boddy and the body that had been placed in the chair. "Jan, Fetch Abby and Mary, bring with them some water in a bowl and some clothes. This man is injured and eats with us tonight." Sebastian sat still and placed his free hand on his lap, he listened to two of them speak in his world of darkness and then to the footsteps of the woman as she walked away to fetch the others. He was left in his own silence for a few moments while he listened to the cracking of the fire in front of him. The odd ember would rest on his foot and singe him slightly but rather than complain he just endured the pain with all the other wounds he had on his body. His head still throbbed from days of not being able to eat or sleep properly. The sounds of the fire soothed him slightly and within a few moments, he hung his head to stretch his neck, moved it quickly and cracked part of his shoulders letting out a huge sigh of relief. Durk was sleeping off two large pairs by uniting longs laces and threading them through holes, lace by lace, action by action. Once he had finished he pulled the boot from his foot and let it crash to the ground with a mighty thud. After a few moments, he pulled the other off and stretchered his legs out in front of the fire. Boddy had gone off somewhere and left the two men alone in the room. Durk observed the old blind man sitting in the chair next to him. "These wounds are not self-inflicted" old Sebastian said, feeling the gaze of Durk bury into all the corners of his skin. "I shan't need clothes, or medical attention or gold. I shall just need what I have on me for now and if you can spare, some food to rebuild me. I have been like this for a long while." Durk stared stunned at the blind man, he pulled a pipe from his pocket and filled it with buckwheat from a box in front located just above the fireplace and used a long piece of wood to set alight in the fire before awkwardly lowering it into the pipe to light. He took some puffs out of and blew the spoke above him over them both. "Would you be needing some pip?" said Durk offering the pipe to Sebastian while stretching out his great arms. "No need" replied the blind man, "I never touch what can be turned to vapour, nor have I placed my hands on any beer for a long time." He remembered the days at taverns and drinking from large tankers. "I have to lead a simple life for some time now. It has been quite a while since I had felt the warmth of a fire on my face. For this, I thank you and your kindness." Durk took a long drag on his pipe and exhaled another puff of smoke in the air. "We Burchers are known for our hospitality and such, would have been a fool's errand to leave you on that hill anyway. Brylan would have had hell to pay with us. I have needed to appease him enough this day in." Both men faced the fire, one staring into it while the other had no eyes to stare with. After a few moments, two young ladies walked into the room, one carrying a bowl of water and some clothes for Sebastian, the other just carrying the symptoms of being pregnant. "Hallo Husban" She said while the other stayed quiet. She walked over to Durk and kissed him while he sat in his chair, placing one hand on his should and the other on her swollen belly. "Mary, ave you been cookin' with Jan all day? Bet you been cookin' up a storm?" "I ave my husban. By the way, remember. Tonight it's Ennas turn for the trail," "now Jan said she would sing the hymns while you two be at it." Durk placed his head on the belly of Mary and simply said softly "I know", The other woman, Abby simply stood in the room quietly looking down and holding the bowl of water in her hands. Her cheeks stuck out, red and carried all the evidence that she had been crying all day. Her blue eyes had been tinted red while her lips happened to be three shades lighter than they had some weeks before. She was a small girl, standing in a position that made her seem even smaller than she already was. Keeping her head low and trying not to start crying again. "Who is this?" Mary spoke, pointing a long finger at Sebastian, her voice disturbing the feeling of unattached gloom that had followed both the women into the room. "My ladies, This is a pilgrim. He needs a night of rest and food for his belly, maybe some ale to help him sleep, but first he needs to have his wounds washed. He's been walking for days and picked up a few marks on him along the way." Mary stared at Sebastian with squinting eyes. She didn't want to sully her hands with the black marks that might come off the skin of Sebastian or had the chance of his blood being anywhere near her unborn baby. "Abby I need to check with Jan about Supper. It is stew tonight. Can you start on this poor beggar?" she moved towards the kitchen and pasted the doorway leaving Abby to lower down to her knees and place the bowl of water on the floor. She placed the cloth in the bowl and soaked it through, lifted it out and drained it out. Seeing Sebastian's hand resting on his knee she asked him "Can I take your hand, your knuckles ave a few deep cuts on them". Sebastian raised his hand in the air as a sign she may, and she gently pulled it in front of her and started cleaning the dirt from his cuts. The old blind man didn't show any signs that he was feeling any discomfort from these actions and without any objections he had finished wiping down his left hand and above the wrist. Her Gentle actions had been welcomed by Sebastian but thinking it would have been prudent to mention out loud, he just stayed quiet keeping his head towards the fire, not making a move. "Mary" Durk raised his voice as to be heard in the next room. "Can you bring supper in here when it is ready? Make sure the pilgrim gets one too and bring a spoon" His loud voice shook the room and brought a powerful shock to the thoughts of Sebastian, he wished he could just leave the home, but it was dark, there were wolves and he needed food. The staff had rested on his shoulder for a short time now, not pulling him towards any destiny at the moment, he felt it now in some detail. The staff was long, with smooth edges on it and two interwound natural parts that swooped from the top to a few inches below. Marks had been left near a place where Sebastian's hand had settled in the groove. His wooden friend had a few chips at the bottom made most likely by stones resting on the ground. He also felt some writing resting on the handle in a scrip he was yet to identify. Abbey kneeling on the floor waited patiently for him to finish his movements and then began to clear blood from his other hand that would not let go of the wooden director. Durk raised from his chair, "I'm going to visit the privy, You be okay alone? Abbey, don't you run off now, ya hear." The young lady nodded as Sebastian had raised his hand as an act of compliance. The large feet of the man seemed to make more noise with his boots removed and his body walked with less control as he exited the house and braced the evening air. The cracking of the fair resumed being the superior sound in the room and Sebastian sat calmly while the moves of the young lady cleared the dirt from his wounds. A small whisper came from below him and he turned his head to hear better. "Did he say anything?" "Who" he answered to the voice hoping to catch every word as of its faintness. "My husban, did he say anything before" she swallowed the sadness that she felt before and she sealed it inside herself. "He said a few words offering the man to Brylan", she suddenly spoke up "not him. He is not my husban yet." It became apparent that Sebastian was speaking with not the wife of Durk but the man who now resided on the hill. "Ey, he already drew his last breath when I had arrived. I am sorry I was not able to capture what he was like. I believe he faced his fate bravely and refused to shed his dignity." Both remained silent for a while after his words. She rose the cloth filled with water and rubbing against The old blind man's head with some force holding as much sadness back inside herself as she could. He accepted her pressure without a word, he knew she was not angry at him, but the world and how she would accept it was this way. She rinsed the cloth in the water, waited for a second and looked at the blind man. She breathed before saying. "I am very sorry about this, the pain I feel and I thank you for listening to what I am about to say." The young women placed the cloth in the bowl and spoke to Sebastian for a short while. "I must be quick before he returns, I cannot say the name of my husban again every. He was a good man, just not capable of what was chosen of him. He only wanted me but to have me he needed others too. The others are being given away soon, I have been arranged here but I still miss him, he was so kind and yet they didn't even let me say goodbye. I am his widow and I will be remarried next week." Sebastian held his words to him and all he could do was listen to the poor woman, her heart had been damaged and she was now going to continue without the man she loved. The noises of Durk headed back towards the doorway, he walks through and heads to the kitchen. She looks up at Sebastian, "we are not allowed to say his name." Sebastian understood and Abbey picked up the bowl, raised it to her feet, bowl in hand and walked towards the kitchen. Sebastian sat in his darkness as Durk walked his way towards the old blind man. "She helped you a lot she did" His bellowing voice disturbed the sound of the embers Sebastian had enjoyed so much. He felt a mug being placed into his hand and he took a sip from it. Strong, very full beer made its way into his mouth. He sipped it well but did not speak a word. "Once the season comes for it, she'll be making Cidre my Jan. That's if the baby gets delivered on time, if not she will be the midwife." Sebastian took another sip from the mug placed in his hands. The liquid was warm, sloping around when he lifted the mug to his lips and hushed the headache that came with the words the turned towards him from Durk. After some time Mary entered into the room with two bowls of stew in hand. The Smile from Durk could not be contained and when the bowl was placed onto a piece of wood that he had across his lap he looked for a spoon. Mary placed it lovingly into his hands with pride that she was the one to do so. He plunged his spoon into his stew and reached a large potato to his lips covered in brown liquid. It burned his lips and he opened his mouth, blowing out of it while trying to cool down the entire inside. Mary gazed over him with delight. She was proud he was her husband and that she would have his child growing inside her and that she would be bearing it for him. She turned her head and then forced her gaze on old Sebastian. This beggar looking of a man was sitting enjoying a fire with her husband, leaving black footprints below him and fowling the air around him. "How dare he" the words rattled in her head. "How dear this beggar walks into our home and takes what is ours to give. Our hospitality. Our comfort. He doesn't belong here." The words echoed in her head, she looked down on the bones covered in skin, the wounds that had been cleaned by Abby, the walking staff clutched in one hand and the rags that hung from his frame. She didn't go to hear him but as was the will of her husband, who now was spooning large quantities of hot stew into his mouth, burning his tongue further. She took a few steps towards him, and a quiet voice arose from the living amount of withered flesh and stitched eyes. "Can you place the bowl in my lap, please and would you kindly place the spoon in the bowl on the left side." she balanced the bowl on his legs with only his rags protecting his legs from the heat of the bowl, it radiated his skin and the wounds on his legs ached a little. Looking forward, Sebastian felt around the bowl to get a better idea of where it was in the world. Mary held the spoon in her hand, It was slightly bulky and made of wood, a smooth texture that had been carved by someone in the village. She looked down at the beggar with a look of injustice on her face and slid the spoon under the surface of the stew. It sank out of sight in a few seconds. A smile came over Mary's face with the accomplishment of her petty act. "Oh, I'm sorry", she said with a slight smirk, "let me get you another one". She had no intention of bringing another and hoped it would burn the old blind man. Sebastian knowing the tone in her voice spoke up from his silence with a pittance in his voice. "I will not worry about that," he said while hovering his hand over the bowl. He slipped his fingers into the stew and with great discomfort, he pulled the spoon from the bowl and brought it to his lips. Licking his fingers clean to the best of his ability Sebastian would not waste any part of what came out of his bowl and made sure not to lose one part. Mary looked at him with content and turned walking towards the kitchen, where the others sat and ate. The Stew its self was pleasant enough. A brown bowl made of some sort of ceramic texture, decorated with markings on it that in some way resembled leaves, it had likes drawn into the side to help the grooves of the fingers keep hold of it and formed a circular base at the bottom. Inside was a thick watery brown sauce, holding close to carrots that had been chopped down their sides, potatoes that had been skinned, chopped, boiled and then placed in the soap which small green peas that floated with the rest of the vegetables. With all the ingredients that had been placed in the stew, Sebastian noticed something resistant against his teeth. Was this meat? He had not had it for so long, the flesh fell away as he bit straight into it and which every spoonful he took to his lips he blew to stop the heat from burning him. "what meat is?" this he asked

Durk. The bigger man spoke without raising his head from the bowl and scraped the last amounts of the juice that he could get from the bottom of the bowl. "Chicken, that will be that last one of the season, methinks. Food has become kinda ruff Brylan not being pleased and all." The old blind man blew on his spoon and placed another piece of chicken stew in his mouth. "Why you blow it?" Durk spoke interrupting the one meal the old man had liked the taste of in so long. "It lessens the heat so I don't burn myself, have you never tried it?" Durk looked down at the empty bowl he thought a second and replied with "That wouldn't work, not by a long shot I say." Sebastian smiled to himself. These Burchers were set like fence posts in their old ways. They didn't change for much. Tending the fields and spreading children across the lands, they worked in the day and drank and had children in the night times while observing the rituals of the gods of fertility and then on their passing had to be placed in the grounds. None really questioned the earth, but some at least were kind enough to give an old man a drink and some nourishment for his long day. The night was not too long and while the two men spoke, they drank mugs of beer and continued until Boddy wished them both goodnight and Durk went to perform his duties with his wife Ennas while the others could hear him reach an effort in the house. Sebastian placed the bowl on the floor next to his chair, stretched his feet words the fire and rested, staff in hand. The warmth from the fire and the beer in his body made it slightly harder for him to stay awake, and as he felt himself fall lower in the chair his head fell and sleep came over him completely.

The darkness of dreams would never affect Sebastian, the old blind man knew that with every passing dream he was to take, every time his head would fall and he would retreat into his skull would be another time he could live without being eyeless again. In his dreams, he could see, he could walk without the pain that caused him to hobble. He had those who had abandoned him in the past around him, it all fell back to a time before all had turned sour. He knew it was all a dream but it provided some reprieve from the constant awfulness that was his life. Not even the gods invaded his dreams. This long quest will be over and he will be able to find some relief in all of this. If the Gods are true and keep their words then maybe he could get his eyes back. If they were false and this was a clever joke all played on him then he at least rests in the knowledge that there were no Gods, to begin with. Small victories in the world were what he had to take from it and at times when he was unable to think, breath or walk he at least could try and sleep and escape into his dreams. The taste of the stew still filled his soul with comfort and he was transported back to a time when he could enjoy a stew-like the one he had enjoyed this evening. He wanted to be back to the days when meals came to him every night and return to the times when he could rely on his friends to liven up the spirits but his friends were gone and those days disappeared. Before his dream he could relive the stew he felt his right arm tug and the staff pulled him from the dream and woke up in front of the fireplace in the home of Durk. Sebastian remained quiet and got himself together. The staff proceeded to pull him away from the chair and to his feet. After rising he stumbled a few times in silence and then let himself be pulled towards the door. He took one look back and hoped that Abby could find some freedom in her life, but like most of the worshippers of Brylan, they stayed set in their ways and there was no saving many on his pilgrimage to the new gods. He stepped through the fresh hole to be greeted by the morning cold and the brightness from the sun illuminated his skin slightly. He placed a hand in front of himself and took steps outside of the house. The ground was wet. "It must have rained last night," he said to himself. The staff pulled him towards a lane and letting the staff guide his direction and the old man took up his journey once again. Within a few minutes, they had left the village and the ground had hardened again. The sun had hidden around the clouds and while Sebastian walked towards an unknown direction he felt that he must be heading the right way.

Echo Blind

Chapter Six:

Walking across the paths of the forest had been peaceful for Sebastian. The birds were gracing the skies with singing, trees swayed in the wind, not another soul had been met on the path or had spoke up to be met. Sebastian walked with speed in his step now. He had rested, eaten and was not in as much pain as he had been in the past. The road was softer on his feet than the other trails had been and with no obstacles in his way, he had increased his pace for a few miles. His trusted staff followed the path in groves making Sebastian walk with less obstructions to hold up his way. He breathed in while he walked taking in all that he could from the power of nature. While his feet followed the course set out by his wooden friend, he was unawares of the dark clouds that stayed their ways above him. They had been gluttonous in their presents and continued to follow the old blind man on the path way, leading him to his next destination. His fist had not needed to hold on as hard as he had in the past and the bones in his fingers had been aloud to return to a colour similar to before he had started. His wounds had not desired to spurt blood from their positions and to him, the world had turned around. Unaware of the large grey skies that had silently arrived above him Old Sebastian started to turn his mind what he would have to do with his life once his pilgrimage had ended. He was unable to stop walking once the staff had started pulling him towards the destined journey and Old Sebastian had thanked his luck that he had not to cross a river yet and hoped that the hills he had to climb would be his last. He had felt a hunger come across his mood with no ability to grab food at this moment he thought to him what was the likeliness of him receiving his next meal soon. Over the last few days during and before the long travel, he had not eaten much but had gotten by on what he was able to scrounge. The churches wouldn't take in the old blind man, nor would they help with his wounds. The charity of helping the poor had not been offered to him for his words, spoken on street corners, reached from the top of boxes used to carry supplies. If he had a way he would deliver his message loudly and from those remarks that came from below his tongue, deep down his gullet, beyond the bowls of fury that sat in his heart, he disturbed members of the religious communities, orphanages, helpers of the poor and misfortune, and even those who worshipped the more destructive gods. In the beginning he drank, he drank so much that his body had become numb and his mind had softened to the world and to a point that the pain cast from the bottoms of his souls would not bother him. Then after he was plunged into the forever darkness he found it less available to quench his thirst with the poisons he had used to lessen his feelings, but still the bile came out of his mouth and with instances of screams and shouts he called out the central squares until he was beaten and told to move on. He called his words to the passers by in the streets and alleys from door ways and steps. Still he had stones thrown at him, fists raised to him, his shoes stolen by the worshippers of greed. His anger never faded, it just rested in moments when he could not keep up the energy and after the pain he had experienced, he realised in with his own facts that their was no gods to begin with.

"If their was gods of any kind, couldn't they show their power to man, could they not stop the disasters that left many dead, homeless and diseased. Speaking of diseases, why do children die of horrible plagues that render them crippled from the inside. Why is there spores that turn animals to mindless drones or parasites that leave the old delirious? Why do the old lose their minds to age and some are left to wander the streets with no reliance but to be abused and destroyed? Why do the gods allow people to go through what he did?"

He was now in the forever black, still being pulled around by a piece of wood with a mission of its own. Now they had decided to raise their mighty minds and give the one man who didn't believe a task so he could then believe. "Well there are no gods" the conclusion he came to still in his mind. While he walked locked in his own mind, the clouds grouped above him and grew larger and larger in the sky, becoming darker while the day grew longer. Old Sebastian felt his joints yearn and his legs start to stumble at points but still he decided to think inside this darkness, using the time alone to reflect on what had happened. While his path continued the heavens opened and rain slowly fell towards the grown while increasing in number. The grooves in the path were the first to fill with water, then footprints left by might beasts and before long small streams had built up in the unhurried striking sunlight.

The old man raised his head and finally realised that it had been raining for a while and his rags and robes were getting soaked through. His face felt the keen rain, flowing from his drawn eye sockets and slightly stinging his features. I followed the path laid by his wrinkles and gathered in areas that adsorbed all the liquid that fell from the sky. It started to shower and he accepted his fate to be cold and sick again. With little nudges his path was slightly altered and the wooden staff pulled him towards the trees for ample shade. There he was allowed to stop slightly as the staff went motionless and remained steady in the journey. He leant on the wooden friend and lifted his chin expelling the excuse from his being. His morning start had let him travel miles before the midday and now his body ached from need of rest. His life had passed the time of excitement and at his age he should have been waiting for the hand of the end to guide him peacefully into the afterlife. He was waiting for the day that his mind would stop, his thoughts would run dry and his eyes would close forever. Death was not something he feared at this moment. He had made his peace and with the idea that nothing happened but his body would be a meal for wild dogs or insects amused him. He smiled into the blank darkness with unknown intension. It had been so long since he had last seen something outside his own mind that he no longer missed the sunrises. They always came and never went way, the heat always swelled by midday in the summers and was unbearably cold in the winters, he never wanted to know what season it was, nor did he inquire the look

of the people around him. He guessed he hadn't
looked as he did the last time he gazed in a mirror,
feeling the marks on his face it had become more
evident that his exhausted features had become more
considerable as the awareness it had been made to
him by his weary joints. Sometimes his legs shacked
when he stood and he in the past had not being able to
move from the hovels he had made for himself in the
street corners to shelter him from the environment
and passers by. The spaces between his finger nails
had slipped, revealing deep wounds that if pressured,
they would divert a white thick mucus out and would
run down the racks in his knuckles. His skin would
flake off in parts and the rest would turn to sand when
he rubbed concentrated partitions. He felt tired. His
head would fall slightly but he needed to continue.
What was this all for, a quest into darkness to a land
he knew not, being lead by an object that did not
speak but had a mind of its own and would not let
him release his grip. Leaning on the staff he puzzled
in his skull on whether he would be able to snap his
fine friend. The fiend was thin in some cases but
seemed to be made of a well composed wood. His
curves and etched features seemed to be crafted to the
point of vigour and with all the weight Sebastian was
limited to place into the staff it would not break.
There seemed to be no weak points, nothing to hack
at without tools. It stood well against the mud with
defiance to the elements around. "maybe I should
have placed an end in the fire" old Sebastian thought
to himself. Seeing if the fires would have been kind to
the staff was a particular thought to bear but from this
moment the staff seemed to notice the down pour was

easing up and pulled the old man from his rest, towards the continued destination.

"Darkness, fear and blight are my allies, my friend. They scheduled my days well, and   placed inside me enough chaos to keep me from any journeys in my life. It has come to no   surprise to me with this affliction that I would be left in the streets with no real help and with   my attention cast onto the passers around my misery. I should have expected to be left to fade into the void of this world. But you, you came for me and still unable to speak to me as   another should, you have taken it onto yourself to guide me towards the destinations tricked on me. If I only have this what should I have any more? I am not deserving of bread or meat, defiantly not the ambition of one such as yourself."

His words had been sent, hollow to the world around him without as much of a plan but the first step he could he turned his body quickly and tried to run in the opposite direction. This action failed promptly as his fist tightened on the staff, his back stiffened and the staff stopped in the middle of the past. Old blind Sebastian pulled with all his might away from the strong wooden friend but he could not over power it. "I will" But he was unable to finish the words from his mouth as the staff lifted slightly in the air and leaned forwards, forcing him to follow. His arm bought the full baring of pain in the sockets and with the his fingers clenched to the point of his digits becoming white hot. He wanted to refuse this task, being dragged towards lands he would never be able to see. Twisting his body some more now and using his legs coiled round his knees he pulled away from the staff, using the tendency left within his presence but again the staff stood still in static moments and waited for him to ease up on the pulling to fight back. He called out, using his throat to release the exasperation from his body. He shouted uncomprehending slurs into the sky out of frustration but nothing vexed him more than the staff just waited in silence for him to let up on his incessant pulling. Old Sebastian slipped his feet falling to his knee and the staff started to pull his right arm towards the destination they were taking before Sebastian's rebellion. Slowly Sebastian was dragged forwards until he gave into the wooden guide and tried his hardest to hobble in a way that satisfied his presence. He had been defeated by an object that had been placed with more trust than the gods had given to humanity. It that was to be believed of course. He breathed quickly trying to recapture the life that had escaped him with that escapade. Drops of sweat replaced the cool rain drops that had filed on his face and with that he now followed the path that had been set out for him. "Darkness, fear and blight are my toughest alleys my friend but you scare me more." he spoke to the staff but no reply followed. Just the continuation of the journey ahead as footsteps made foot prints in the path.

Chapter Seven:

"We give ourselves for you our mighty goddess, for you will guide us to the light." The voice of a woman could be heard, The voices carried over the fields and went past the normal stops to be noticed on the but not to be seen. "She, who takes from all and bestows onto those who she sees fit, we, her followers shall offer onto her the gifts to win her favour." Old Sebastian felt the words on his ears and tried to stop in his flow of walking but the wooden staff pulled him strongly, making him stumble forward and he no longer felt hard dirt, or soft mud under his feet but the blades of wild grasses being trampled under his way. The voice of the woman echoed its way outward and was only unbalanced slightly by the trees around that swayed gently in the wind. The staff pulled the old man further and further, his feet came in contact with leaves, roots of trees, fallen trunks and his enjoyment of a relatively uncomplicated road and no sharp objects had been traded from the beginning of an untamed forest. The staff pulled him further and further, deep into the forest as the journey started to trip Sebastian. "Calm yourself" the old man shouted "I am old and blind, I cannot keep up with your jerks and I will fall." Speaking to the wood as if it had ears to be placed with his words. The escalation of pace started to tire the old man. His breath had become heavy, while his steps began to falter. He found himself needing to fall but with the strength and pace of his wooden friend, his movements never faltered and he stirred into the forest placing his hand on a non introduced tree every so often to steady himself. His lack of vision waisted the beauty around him as green gave way to browns, reds and oranges. The floor had been laid with plants of colours unbound, veins deep blue and small purple petals, gently hiding from the mockery of hooves trampling them to oblivion out of fright. Sebastian had not seen a forest such as this, nor would he ever see it again. His dark world was not forgiving enough for him to find solace in the visual aspect that grips one's heart to flutter. He had tended the fields in his past, he had hidden in forests beyond and foraged to survive the ravages of hunger that had been laid upon him in his adolescences. He had felt thorns break the skin of the souls of his feet but he kept on, further as to how long the staff would take him. His feet felt unsteady but rather than fall to the ground under the tired weight of his body, they continued the stride and helped enforce his journey further. The staff struck roots, dug into mounds and pinned all matter to the ground on its way towards the unanswered destination. "Your vigour is weighing on my patients." Old blind Sebastian shouted towards his arm, hoping in some moment he would be able to stop but alas the staff pulled him, as he should continue to collide with tree trunks and his head would get tangled for slight moments in branches and spider webs. The voice of the women before had now gone silent but had been replaced with another, spouting off with her own style of worship towards the greatness of this female god. "She has always delivered what delightfully is called gifts and she has always..." The voice was stumbling trying to make up some sort of worship poem while still delivering. The voice was unable to conceal the presence of anger and this seemed to misguide the speech further. Her voice began to tremble slightly and after a deep breath and slight silence she started again. "blessed be the name in which we bow before. Blessed be the joys in our hearts through worship. Blessed be her who guides us towards the rightful way of worship. She who gives us to covet. She who gives us to have…" The voice picked up confidence and beamed with pride over its newfound confidence. Sebastian hoped his journey could be broken soon and as his steps grew slower and slower, the voices grew closer and louder. He had felt the soil beneath him become less covered in thorns and twigs and unknowingly he found himself in a clearing. The trees formed an unconsecrated barrier between the clearing and the outside world. The soil felt soft. The wind blew gently and now the staff pulled old Sebastian with less power than it had moments ago. Sebastian let his footsteps grow quiet and glided with his wooden friend until he came to a stop. Wasting no time he caught as much of his breath as he could, bent over to his knees and hoped for his life force to return quickly, all the while listening to the mantras of the two voices ahead of him.

The clearing was not large, nor small but instead, it was enough. The trees around hung towards the centre, trying to grab with their branches whatever seemed to be out of reach in the area. All manner of natural life had stopped growing, giving an eerie sensation with on this day no shade from the sunshine and more recently little defence against the rain. The soil seemed to prove some stability to the old blind man, but he felt his feet sink slightly into the dirt with not much resistance. The sweat from his bold head fell onto the ground forming puddles for only a few seconds and then disappearing into the rich black soil. Standing in the middle of the sacred space was a large stone shrine. The clearing provided some strange focus point for the shrine while it was carved the silky legs of a goddess moving playfully in a static position. The stone had been made smooth after years of being available to the elements and the harsh rains of the autumns provided an amount of life which was used to great effect by this worshipped stone slab. The smooth stone legs led up the grey slab to a body positioned steadily on top, seated and lead to curves of a woman's body that bore two it six arms. Each arm lead stretched out towards the spaces around the shrine and had objects of significance to many of its worshippers. The lowest arms held clutched inside their hands two gourds said to contain the finest wine, beer and spirits of the lands. The left hand above that held a scythe, ready to cut the neighbours wheat and in the right was the blade of defence, to protect what was theirs. Both tools seemed to have details of wicker handles carved into the hilts and the blades had been flattered in places to show the sharpness of the tools held in the hands of the goddess. The hand above laid flat outstretch just about the head of the goddess and placed balancing was a small object that the image of the goddess seemed to place one half an eye on it, to keep safe for all the time it was to rest in her hands. The object seemed to be a small incense holder, detailed with star patterns, delicately marked and given such beauty as to make sure they had the knowledge of the goddess, so they too could be praised. The top of the trinket had a small loop on top with such detail that a thread could be looped through and be tied around the neck of anyone. The last hand held up high with three fingers a coin, leaving the last two outstretched in a particular fashion. This hand gesture would be the symbolism that the followers of this goddess would use to recognise each other and be used before some prayers. The coin itself had carved into the stone the number one, with a script that if Sebastian still had his vision he still would not be able to read, a script unknown to most, even the followers of her. Garnished on the goddesses head was three long sets of beads. Placed on her head by her followers to symbolise her wisdom and cunning, while her body was wrapped in the fabrics not to be worn by any human. Her feet had been painted with the juices of local plants, displaying patterns formed by dots. These patterns had been drawn on the knees as well as marked on the plinth itself, covered in circler markings that spanned each other and had lettering floating above the form. These lines are made of geometric sophistication, that would have the ability to make adores falling towards it in unison, deep into a hallucinogenic recreation. Many of the devotees at the shrines such as this would move their heads to the sky, crossed their arm's and leaned towards their knees while not being able to piece together their own conclusions. after they would lay their hands in front of them and fall to the ground with force, placing their foreheads violently on whatever was lining floors, housing these shrines, depicting the goddess, while stretching their hands out forming the same gestures as the hands of the shrine before them. After a few moments, one worshipper would raise their heads and shout praise at the statue of their deity. Then another worshipper would rise and filled with jealousy in their hearts would try to out compliment the words said before. This act was being performed by the two women in the clearing before the old man's non-working eyes, while both had been hunched over, one now stood to her feet and placed an item before her in offering to the silent idol before them. She then laid her face to the soil below her and stretched out her arms again, placing her fingers in the style as the hand that head the coin that firmly was above her. "I am blessed to offer this to you, Divine all-powerful guider towards the light." she called out, her words seemed to be made up while she chanted in a crouched position. Fingers still stretched. The Second woman, moved her shoulders up first, letting her arms fall to her sides and placed one foot in front of her to let her knees gain the strength of her body. She kept her head low and while looking towards the ground she fumbled, searching a cloth bag that hung off her shoulder and had several items hidden inside of it. Her hands rolled around inside for some seconds while she seemed to be in deep thought. In a panic she raised her head, looking down one of her shoulders and she finally found what she was to offer the silent goddess. The object so delicately cupped in her hands was a small bell, covered in lettering hand-carved in such a way to see the metal was scratched with blunt tools. She had a smile on her face under her bowed head and was then ready to breathe in and speak out the words of offering to the goddess statue. She held her breath, looked up and lost all her saved intensity. "The bell" the words passed her lips with defeat in the air. Sebastian could hear her say, "The bell" two times under her breath. On the ground, at the foot of the shrine was another, bigger bell. The offering was made of less compressed metal, dotted with fewer scratch marks and made with a wooden handle, unlike her metal one. She let her bell chime a frequent number of times in the breeze that had been picked up at the moment, before placing it some steps away from the first, bigger bell. She then laid her head to the ground, hands outstretched as of the style brought about before. She then exhaled what little breath she had inside her, gathering from the pit of her stomach. She spoke loudly "Yena, I offer you this bell, may it chime for you musically and soothe your days, please let it be that in which you seek." Her words, rang of hope, hope that she would be recognised in the divine light of her ever amounted dryad. The name Yena swirled through the air and favoured its way towards the ears of old Sebastian. He had heard that name before, but not in the style of the greater gods. Far from it, Yena had a reputation between followers of other gods, beasts and mystics. Stories had arisen from villages and towns. Though once they had temples built in many cities west of two of the great rivers, their temples had been hidden in secrets these days. Many of their followers out of control with their desires had their faiths driven underground and to find a shine in this size had been such a rare event as to find the gods themselves. Yena's followers had taken entire houses from villages, spent vast fortunes of gold, destroyed entire merchant caravans and plunged a few empires into darkness while burning their subjects alive. The main adherence of her believers was that wants needed to be taken. No object, event or act was taboo to be copied and it must be done greater and better. Clothes could be ripped from backs, spouses could be stolen or murdered by coveting companions. Friends turned to enemies and villages turned to dust. The skilled in some cases had been executed by having fingers hacked violently and unskilfully in public. Most outsiders rightfully treated this faith with contempt and suspicion as these devoted persons used not only their doctrines to justify some odious acts. Crops, jewels and lovers had been stolen in her name. Wars and famines had been dedicated to her and her worshippers smiled just to be basked in the thought of her everlasting glow. She was Yena, the Goddess of Jealousy, a Spectre of envy, a vision of the jaundiced eye. Rivers had been poisoned in the name of jealousy, for the sight of beauty should never be compared.

Goddess had been know to deal out punishments in her name and from the allowed scripts that detailed her deeds to show the way to her followers it had been filled with fables to be taken in context. One such tale focused on the princess from some lands far away from the very spot anyone had told it. It began with the world adoring the princess of a kingdom.

The reach of the kingdom stretched far and wide with many rivers, hills, mountains and cities all in between. Yet as far as the kingdom went it was known that the princess had the beauty for all the lands. She was the most allure in all the land and could not be compared with any woman who fell under her shadow, and yet she had eyes, only eyes for one man in this world. He was a handsome gentleman of the lower barons, and with that made him unfit to marry such a woman of high standings. He loved her so but so knew he was not respected enough. One night while drunk, he walked the lands that he owned, tripping on the stones beneath his feet. Yena heard his prayers for salvation to be delivered to his devoted princess. "Why?" he called out, "why is she not in my arms? moral standing to be. We are in love and that should be more than enough. How? How can I prove she should be mine and live forever in happiness." The grin on the goddesses face was enough to change the sky into a bedazzlement of stars. "A deal o'yes a deal was to be hatched on a night of this calibre". Yena appeared above the man, flitted slightly behind one of his ears and spoke gently to him. "What is your plight handsome sir?" she said with not a delusion towards how the young man looked. "Oh great voice from the heavens," he said without fear. "The princess of these lands and I am her rightful suitor." Yena had a plant growing inside her. "Land, that is what you need. Noble birth is in you but if you can grow your influence through the land you will show your power and then no one could deny you the future you desire with your love." The young man didn't see the game the goddess was playing with him. "Of course" he called out. "I will gain land and then once I have enough I, we shall be married and that should be all that I need from then on. Her and me forever, that is all." "Really," The goddess said with all the intention of the playfulness of vandalism in her voice. "I find that once you have a square of land, it will never be enough, you will all ways yearn for more and more and love will never be enough or the love of your princess." The young man disagreed and in the morning after he woke, he set about acquiring land. Soon his estate stretched out further than his eyes could see. He bought up what he could from the surrounding barons, those who had come into debt and those who could no longer afford the upkeep of the fields. We went to auctions and bought out those lots that had become unacquainted. Soon he had more cows, chickens, horses, fields and serfs working on them to know what to do and yet this was not enough. He had brought enough land to his power to be noticed by the king, but it was not enough to him. He was brought respect, accordances, titles with the more land he acquired and after some time, he was allowed into more of the respected banquets he was not allowed to attend because of his status. Soon a wedding day was set for him and the princess but

yet he was not satisfied with what he had. He looked
to his neighbours and took their lands in ways of
punishment and false treason. The gold he had
inherited from these acts fuelled his greed and yet he
looked towards what he ate with and it was not
enough. He wanted bigger castles in the land. He
looked at barons the same as himself and wanted their
houses, their robes, their favours. Soon he was
married to the princess and was granted endless
power and yet. He looked at the land of those around
him. Some barons had more fertile lands, while others
had forests of the tastiest fruit. This would torment
him in his sleep and he heard the voice of Yena. "It
should all be yours." He looked towards his father in
law. The King had lands, power, castles, the best of
meals. He had all that the young man earned for. Now
he found himself watching the King and wanting the
same stretch of influence he had. Jealous set in and
night after night he laid awake imagining himself
one-day being king. After some time the king fell ill
and the young man went to work with his wanting.
One night the princess drunk on brandy wine went to
sleep early and in the pure rage of jealousy, the young
man went to the room of the king and sliced his
throat. With the blood from the knife, he smeared it
on the princesses clothes and blamed her for the
murder. With this act, he became king and assumed
the kingdom. Thus the twisted morality of the story,
anything that is wanted should be taken. Yena, The

Goddess of Jealousy, is the fuel for all desires and with her divinity, her followers will pursue until oblivion catches them. The Stories had been shouted out loud by the merchants, flogging gems at the markets Sebastian had slumped himself near in fits of tired cessation. The Gems, pendants, idols and related artefacts of Yena were strictly taboo in this but still, they fetched a high price and thus they would be sold. The prayers had grown silent in front of old Sebastian enough for him to be brought out of his thoughts. He felt eyes burning their desires on him and his rags had somehow become heavier.

The two women seemed dressed in better robes than most. Both had long pieces of cloth cut in measures and draped down, only stopping at the ankle. Each measure had an amount of texture sewed into the fabrics and both had some brighter colours. One robe was made of soft material and was mostly blue with colours of green and brown stained with some sort of organic dye. It somehow gleamed in the light and looked light enough to provide a cooling sensation on hot days and protection from the winds on colder days. The other women had a similar garment on but were coloured orange and red with markings on it that formed the pattens quiet like the birds of the east. Each woman had not worn shoes but instead made a point of leaving them at the entrance to the clearing and had pieces of soil clumped to their knees, but

both of their bare feet had been kept well and from
that their bodies had not seen acts of war or hardship
in the same manner as those from the lesser classes
the estates they had clearly come from. Yet in acts of
faith they had left their servants behind and walked
the lands without horses but what could have been
worn on their selves was to be shown. Before this
day, each woman had stolen the others offerings with
calls of jealously and instead offered what they had
presented to the idol of Yena. They had seen each
other's gifts or paid for information on the other as to
upstage the value of the offering and create more
jealousy in the process. With this, the garments of
both women had been practically picked as to create
the most jealously in the other woman, just to be
looked at favourably by the goddess. It was malarious
to see to the common eye but old Sebastian was none
the wiser of what they were wearing and instead
focused on the feeling in the atmosphere around him.
Both women rose to their feet and slowly walked
towards the blind man. Was he Yena in disguise to
test the faith of both, clearly not but he had an owe
about him that lead to both of the praying women to
stop their rituals and approach the blind man? The
staff pulled him slightly forward but more to ready
him and as the air around him grew tighter, the old
man swallowed the breath in his presence and stood
steady in the clearing. "What is this? The woman in
blue spoke out loud. "Surely we have been blessed

with a mysterious stranger" The woman in orange replied. Sebastian stood with the old wooden friend in hand and keeping quiet. Old Sebastian kept quiet and his head pointed towards the ground beneath his feet. The darkness he was perpetually in showed him no visions as to who was approaching him but the two voices he heard came unaccompanied and suggested footsteps towards him. He could h/ear bare feet moving earth with movements readying decent. His robes felt pulling from his elbows and back and he smelt slight perfumes from soaps in the air. He felt hands caress over his wooden staff while each woman circled him, checking on his wears as to secrets they could offer their goddess. "What brings you to our shrine?" the voice of the woman in blue sounded into his ears loudly. Old Sebastian spoke quietly letting his voice fade slightly into the wind. "I am just on a pilgrimage, I must travel the lands from where I must visit the lands to the east". Both women seemed to stop their circling but keep their beady eyes over the torn shall of the old blind man. His reply had not settled well with both of the women and as he breathed somewhat carefully, both had left their hands on his person. "Your staff," said the woman in orange, "Why do you clutch it so?" He felt a soft hand placed above his and the slight playfulness of a little finger. "It was a gift, from someone who cannot replace it." his words made no real sense to himself or both of the women but this did not deter both of them from gently pulling his staff once or twice between purses. The women in blue stood in front of him pulling on the staff gently with playful moments and then pulled Sebastian sharply forward. "This will make a perfect offering to the goddess." she pulled Sebastian towards the shrine with violent motions and looking towards the ground for objects to strike at him, pulling with motions to remove the old man's hand while trying to remove his fingers with the other, she was not in the realisation that for the staff to be shaken from the clutches of the old blind man, that his hand would have to be defiantly removed by the gods that had bestowed the pilgrimage on him. With no warning, the woman in orange jumped at her fellow worshipper and struck her face with her hand. "How dare you try to offer this present to the divine one, I saw it first." her slap had caught the woman in blue off guard and she realised her hand from the staff. Sebastian felt more pulls from his staff but was now moving in any direction that was freely made. He felt force around him and the sound of two bodies falling violently to the floor. Both of the women forced each other into the dirt with mindless jealously. Sebastian heard their violent acts, words and force all around him and his perception of where to place his feet or which direction to go had been compromised. He started stepping in a few paces towards him as the loud thud of bodies indented the air around his feet. The staff pulled him diagonally away from the spitting burdens in front of him and after a few steps, he felt the strap of a bag that had become loose in the exchange. He tried to walk away but the staff pulled him towards this object and after a few turns her felt it at his feet, picked it up with one hand and threw it down his arm and over his shoulder. He then felt the full strength come deep inside him being delivered from fear and the staff pulled him again towards a direction that he could not see. His feet gave chase behind the new quickness of his wooden friend and the voices from the vile women had been bled out by the thumping of his resolve in his ears.

Chapter Eight:

The staff wouldn't let the old man rest, not a second and with the long journey they had the voices of the women silenced behind old Sebastian's ears until he no longer had to fear the two jealous women breaking his hands to relieve him of the staff. Jealousy is a great sin in this world and was never needed to further the makings of any society but the prospect to bring pleasure to an all-powerful deity always made some moral turn towards a more bloody path and wreaked havoc on many. Followers of the Mushroomites, a group who believed in small imp-like creatures with wings who sprinkled particles of magic on mushrooms of the forest worshipped kindly. They would lead their village peoples into the forests surrounding them and ingest the mushrooms that grew on the floor. The colours of the mushrooms would be a slight pink hue covered in spots of gold flakes. They could all raise the mushrooms above their heads and lower them into their mouths, crush them with their jaws and sallow them into their gullets and from that the true festivities would realise Mass hallucinations would then follow with writings of trees giving the secrets of the forests, or intense spectral visions of winged creatures flying ahead of the followers and dripping the wine of magnesia on their naked bodies. They caused no real harm to anyone, the odd murder by smashing the skulls of

strangers after a bad vision was very rare. The
Mushroomites wanted just to live off the lands and
consume the mind-altering fungi that they believed
had been gifted to them by higher powers, powers
enabling their followers to see past the reality of this
world. One follower came up with an idea, he
collected the sacred mushrooms and pressed them
into a sort of wine. For days and nights, he looked
after the sacred drink and waited for the main festival
of the year. On that day he presented everyone in the
village, from the village elders to the infants who had
their juice to be mixed with milk to make it look more
appealing to the "younglings". The villagers had been
waiting for this in anticipation and could not wait and
when the time was right in that evening the members
of the Mushroomite village consumed the wine in one
big swill, let their hands fall limp to their sides and
never raised them again. It was then realised by those
who discovered the isolated village sometime later
that concentrating the magic fluid of the mushrooms
would lead to a paralysing death. While taking one
bite out of a mushroom would only lead to
hallucinations, altering the methods would lead to
much worse. That story led had been heard by old
Sebastian long ago, it had become legendary around
some campfires, in taverns when the meed had not hit
the right spot. It circled with stories of The Gods of
Lust, The Gods of Drink, The many beasts that
guarded supposed treasures or vineyards around the

lands, across seas and on top unreachable mountains. The thoughts of faith echoed in his mind and while keeping up with his wooden friend, Sebastian grew melancholic with the trails he had walked. He had not saved, convinced or gifted anyone with his appearance in their lives. He had witnessed more suffering reflecting in his darkness than had he saved with mentioning his beliefs or even reviling that he had been given a pilgrimage by those claiming to be new gods of this world. The proof he needed was all in the staff and yet he still did not believe in any of the almighty beings he had heard of or the ones that had in theory spoke to him. He had evidence that they existed and yet he still doubted them. His steps kept placing themselves in quick fashion around tree roots and dead leaves. He required rest but he could not. Not until the staff had decided they had gotten far enough away from the two ladies who shrieked bloody vengeance towards the heavens of paradise just to offer the divine object Sebastian had sealed into his hand. His toes dug into the earth at points and made his calluses hurt more. Some of the rags covered in his blood from before had fallen away, to the ground to be calmed by the forest but he could not stop to retrieve them. He felt the pace in his body give out slightly and almost sensing himself falling to the ground, the staff started to relent on its driven force and slowed down so Sebastian could catch his breath. The old blind man was not allowed to come to a complete stop but he was allowed to walk briskly at a more satisfactory pace. The stitches in his eyes throbbed slowly, as his pulse slowed from its panicked momentum to an even beat. Sebastian in his new state of progress had come to realise he was thirsty. He kept clutched in his hand the bag he had picked up before from the worshippers of Yena and while moving keep to the step that the staff forced him to go, he proceed to throw the strap around his wooden friend and used him to positions in such a way that Sebastian could use his other hand to search it.

The bag itself was made out of clothes that had been stitched together to keep it strong. They had been overlapped stitches in circular directions that met each other over and over to help contain all the contents. It had two colours together of orange and green and the strap had many markings which Sebastian could feel with his fingers. He felt the edge to find the opening and searched the inside. His hand came in contact with a glass bottle filled with wine, he removed it from the bag, thumbed out the cork and placed the neck to his lips. He gasped after drinking, to what seemed like an eternity, and later taking his second swig from the bottleneck used his thumb and first finger to replace the cork in the bottle and placed it back in the bag. He searched with his hands further inside the bag with unsighted touches and found a few slices of thick Manchent cake protected by a well a folded napkin. The cake was sweet and thick covered in the crust, cooked sugar and filled with almonds, enough to leave a slight scent of pleased emotion inside the old blind man's mouth. He broke off a piece with what teeth he had remaining and gummed the rest in an effort to consume his newfound delight. The cake crumbled slightly in his finger with every bite he took. Old Sebastian walked while being guided by the silent wisdom of the wooden staff. He no longer questioned the directions of his silent guide but instead thought of what would be his next experience, what would these so-called new gods think to put in his way? They had been cruel like the old gods, or the mythical beings the old blind man had heard of before. Large mythical gatekeepers to the underworld had more peace on this earth than the two well off countesses. Sebastian himself had found hardships with not believing in the gods. He had received mistreatment for his decisions with blindness, being spat on, starved, humiliated and the pure malice of others seeing has he was not the outcast to the world. The only man on earth that did not believe in one of the many gods that occupied the earth. Why should he care? They only brought to all some form of pain and suffering, forced impregnations or inaccurate ways to deal with surgeries for fatal wounds. Tales of those who worshipped the great ox of the north would bathe their injured worries in the blood of their priced buffalo. Not binding the wounds as was common in the south and those who worshipped the goddess of medicine. Even stranger those know as the Astonests, who sighted time and time again that a powerful being had instructed them to not partake in any of the medications on the earth from the natural roots that grew or even bathe in any slightest. "What was to be brought on would be correct and what will be will be" they mumbled to themselves over and over. Some even died of rotting flesh or after not eating on one of their ridiculous fasts. "Abstinence is the key to being granted the favour of God". Many of those who wished to just live life in prospect with no harm, to be married and with no sour prospects, provide for the families they were to create. Old Sebastian searched the bag some more when able to provide himself with some stability. It was not the wish for the majority of the population of the world to exact revenge on those who did not believe in the same faith as them. Most lived together in harmony and refused to bring violence to those with different beliefs, but fear would grip all once they had seen something that could shake their faith and rather than be punished for not believing they would throw themselves into their faith or find another to convert too. Old Sebastian searched the bag further and felt something small and made of hard metal in the bottom of the bag just rolling about. He placed his finger along with it, then in and out of its hole and again sliding his finger across its smooth surface. He had found a ring, The little object brought him some slight joy. It made a small humming sound as his finger went around and around it, concentrating on keeping his skin as close to the shiny surface as possible. He found a few bumps on it and noticed an imperfection or two. It had a slightly sticky substance on it that would slow down Sebastian's finger as he tried to keep the flow of his pointer consistent. It was a wedding ring he placed his touch upon and with the blind man keeping his face towards the sky the best he can, he gave in completely to the feel of this ring on his skin. He was unable to make out what the small scratches in the metal had said, but it was commonplace for the richer members of society to scratch messages into the metal that would hide into the skin. The joy of having something that provided hope was strange to views of the old blind man if there was any. He had not found much of joy and in searching one bag that two screaming worshippers of Yena, The Goddess of Jealousy had left while letting their envy consume he had received more joy that he had felt after the journey had started, or for sometime before. He was not off-put by owning this item, he played maybe a vision or two of a better-imagined picture of himself, placing in the hands of the couple that had lost the ring and some joy they would experience that he would be able to live in peace setting off one good deed in his later years. It was unbeknown to him that while fingers held the ring between them that he had a red substance rubbed off on them. The ring its self had blood on it and to those who had their sight could see or suspect that the ring's owners would never knowingly have it placed on their persons again, Old Sebastian placed the ring back in the bag, safely in one of the hidden pockets he found, folded a flap of fabric to secure its contents inside and slipped the holder of goods strap over his free shoulder and around his neck. He now was in possession of sweet beads, a ring and something to drink. His journey had been put again on track and he could not hear another being as he placed his footsteps in the forest around him. The rush of blood in his body had numbed the pain of his feet, enough for him to walk in the way with his wooden guide and feel the minimum of pain. Though the knuckles on his hand holding the staff had started to split the skin, from the force of his grip, he was not experiencing the pain that he was used to from it. The Stitches across his eye sockets gave him a gentle tremble to remind him further of the damage to his face but for now, his journey had become bearable.

After some steps and a dwindling pace from Old Sebastian, the roots from the trees stopped knocking the balance of his feet and instead had been replaced by soft grass. The leaves that were falling from the trees became exiguous and the wooden staff made fewer slight detours to miss the forest features. They had made it out, past the forest. No more forest in front of him, just vast plains to walk across with nothing to obstruct him. To the blind man he had survived to come out on the other side and from this, another accomplishment had been reached some sort of unhampered paradise. He lifted his head further to the sky and breathed in, no smells of the forest, or fungi foisting up the era of his senses, or decaying moss, dead animals, insects biting him around his neck and hands, twigs leaving their ingrains on his feet. He came through on the other side with the resistance of the forest and the two worshippers of miss guided goddess. The old blind man had no more worries of these as they were all behind him now. He breathed heavy and felt happy in that notion, smelling the fresh air of the plain that was before him. On the wind, he could hear voices, males with slight cheer, no threats or prayers. Just the voices of men. Sebastian kept walking forward until his foot felt a ridge and the voices could not be mistaken. There he stood, being haunted by the wind, listening to the conversations that continued below him. The valley ahead could be treacherous and what lay ahead was unknown to Sebastian, but with his wooden staff leading the way, maybe he would finally find what he had been set out to do or at least get some food to store for his travels.

Echo Blind

Chapter Nine:

Old Sebastian's steps moved only slightly over the grass, staring into his eternal darkness with nothing more but to listen for voices, carrying on the wind below him, the echoes of laughter coming in, "there must be hundreds" he thought to himself. Heavy noises of metal, crashing to the ground accompanied with the sound of canvas erecting with wooden beams being forced into the ground and with sounds of fingers knocking one after another on timbered places for a string to hold it all together. The advance of his old wooden friend had stopped for now and with the actions allowing for rest, the old blind man sat down, crossed his legs in front of him and let the place of his wooden guide slump on his shoulder. The winds changed direction but still calmly pushed Sebastian to keep himself in a more comfortable position. He did not move after his seat had been taken with stability. He let his head lower slightly and relied on his hearing to assess the situation. Feeling slightly overwhelmed with the unwillingness to indulge in an uneasy company that had been caused by meeting the two women of jealousy, he simply listened and would make his moves into the plain, if the wooden staff so desired it. Sebastian instead started to reflect on his destination. It might have been simpler for the gods to have him swallowed by some great sea beast and then have him vomited onto the beaches close to the destination they wanted him to be at. Then he shook his head and remembered he did not believe in the gods. He did not believe in their stories, he was being played a trick on or some sort of moral dilemma. His thoughts circled his old brain for some time, the sun had set in the time he sat upon the ground and nightfall took over. The smell of fires started in the night filled the aroma of the night sky with warmth and the sound of merry men making their entertainments had replaced the normal tranquillity of the locations routine. The men had set up camps, brought out meats and cooked them over several fires. The sound of cooking meat and cracking tree bark was drained out by the playful discussions of the new travellers that had taken up one night of celebrations before their destination had been reached. The smell of the men on the other hand had been overtaken by the perfumed aroma of cooking meat over fires and barrels of beer being opened and their contents spilling into makeshift goblets followed by toasts and disagreeable slurping sounds and ended with large breaths of comfort. The sounds of chewing arrived after cheers from the cumulation of meat turning tender. The heavy roars of knives slicing down long carvings of meat from whatever animals had once been whole but now had been kissed by flame and fat. These morsels were then hoisted into the air on sharp points and toasted on by their possessors who then followed their actions with the loudest chewing

Sebastian had ever heard. It made him reach for the sugary crumbs sitting in the bottom of his bag in hunger without going for the full piece of the sweet bread, that was to be saved for later. Beer had been the cause of mass slurping sounds in the camp and with hearty conversations, stories and the crackling of wooden fires the night had seemed to allow the prospect of a good night, not too cold and not too hot but complete with a full moon to light the way if the fires died down. Old Sebastian sat biting what was left of the skin on his fingers and rewrapping the rags that once sat on his body, waiting on what the staff had decided to do with their direction. Would it change course or walk right through the camp? Either way, it had made its intention of not engaging the large crowd but instead wished to bide its time. Sebastian himself had welcomed the chance to rest as well as to not be engaged by other populaces. The ones he had met so far had only weighed on his being and now it was time to wait on what the fates would bring into impact. The high moon glowed white into the air with no clouds making their way to cover the brightness and seemed to light the full plain for miles around. The men ignored the calm of the night and had replaced it with the intension of bravado and entertainment.

The voice of one of the leaders burst out, "We have marched many days and after tomorrow we shall march on our desired destination" He placed a tankard to his lips made from the horn of some wild animal. "EY!!" a few voices agreed in the night. "Tamsenal is not a land to be taken lightly" another voice of a prominent elder rang out into the night. "That castle has stood for over four hundred years and with no army making its way to the inside, The dwellers are well defended and supplied to the point that they could and can hold out against all armies including Malfrid's coalition." The voice took one break to sip from his tankard of wood that had been hollowed out, finely and drank from a metal strews that had been fashioned to stand upright, to not lose any of its contents into the beard of the one who drank from it. "Their men are well trained too, not as battle-hardened as ours or the others that shall stand with us in the coming days but trained well enough to hold their own against the short-sighted warriors that follow Raykken," He said before taking another sip of from his tall straw. "Please Arthur, continue with your sullen doubts, for I have not heard enough today from either you or the crows that flew above us our entire march." The other man placed himself firmly on a tree trunk he had positioned himself in a clearing for him to sit close to a very well-fed fire. His beard was unkempt, red and gleamed with the illuminations from the cracking embers that drifted in the nights sky. He had shed his armour and now sat in a white tunic, wearing once glover to keep a grip of his horn, filled with the goodness of man. He smiled at his remark and looked on some of the men close by for his silent applause and laughter. He received some smirks from his company but did not impress the other elder near him, sitting in a chair that had been assembled after the decision to make camp had been made. His verbal opponent, Arthur wore an eye patch, kept his free hand by his side and only unsheathed it to make the odd point while he spoke. His face had been well combed and he spoke with the harmony of knowledge in his voice. Both sat as the opposite of the other, staring around the eyes of each other, while the fire burned bright sending embers into the night's sky. Both leaders of their respective groups of soldiers enjoying what could be their last night of joy before a grim battle, though both had glory on each man's mind. It was never to be put past the other that they would not venture home to celebrate with their townspeople. The old blind man sat in the darkness listening to the words drifting on the night's sky while both men sat with their most trusted warriors, eating and drinking without much care for the presence of someone eavesdropping on their words. "Whether or not the battle goes well I refuse for any other company, but mine own to fight the most valiant and therefore will collect the most gold. I shall bring back a fortune to Esanside and my taverns will grow rich off of me." The red-bearded elder said with high spirits that he refused to give up. Arthur the other elder fished his sip from his goblet and started to bestow his wisdom on the other men, who sat around the fire listening to the verbal sparring of the two leader elders.

"Mazeky, is it only good and glory you have on your actions? Do you not take notes of the political situations? Taking Tamsenal will lead to a shift in the power and that power could be distributed through not only our valleys but the lands to the north, south and east. Gold will be distributed, not only to us but also to main patrons who wish to conqueror these lands. The technology, the gold, manpower from taking this foothold to make a powerful kingdom, an empire in the future even. Sure myself and yourself will be long fallen by the sword when that happens but we, through our descendent might be able to carve out our own dynasty's. It is through these actions that we could engage in the trade routes. Forge ties with our communities, grow and fortifies ourselves, not only our lands but to those who reside as our enemies. From this, we could conquer lands of our own and spread peace."

Arthur sat back in his chair and sipped again at his beverage. Listening to the conversations of the soldiers Mazeky and himself had brought for the long journey to the future he wished to hold. The men around his fire grew slightly silent, making what they could of his words. Arthur had great ambitions, it was evident with not only his words but his manner. Mazeky on the other hand was slightly opposite. He was only concerned with the moments in his close future rather than a far one. His drink in his hand was getting more attention than an idea of a dynasty. He reached for another leg of meat that was cooking on a stick in the fireplace and leaned forward on his makeshift tree seat.

"You think beyond your means Arthur," he said pointing the leg of a cooked animal at Arthur. "We have been hired, we get paid in gold, that is all, we have not an idea of what our employers wish or wish to continue with after our victory. We simply put many to the blade, they fight, we fight, we win, that is the only mission of my men. A fortress needs to be brought down in the world. We have been hired to bring it down. That is our only consideration. I have my hatchet and my sword, my shield is filled with the righteous events of the here and now. I have been hired to bring my men to the edge of battle and lead them straight into it, not only have I agreed to it but I have also given my word."

The camp fell eerily quiet as he spoke his words. The fire in the eyes of Mazeky scorched the minds of those who sat around him. Rather than plan the future of his clan, Makzeky was more concerned about the iron-bound that was his honour. Many looked at him as he spoke with a direct change in his voice. The cheerful bounce that had spared with Arthur's opinions had been replaced with a seriousness brought from years of stepping onto the long plains of battlefields, seeing family and friends standing side by side and engaging in the ideals that they had the righteous efforts pained onto them. Whether in gold or promises, Mazeky still kept his word stronger than the truth and with that, he would deliver on his honour or rest in the next life having failed it. The campfire burned high into the night sky, leaving a line of thick smoke to escape towards the sky. The smell of cooking meat kept the fortunes of the warriors alive with some fortunes to still smile on, but Mazeky's words left a deafening silence that could not be ignored.

"We have no way of influencing the actions of whom so ever offers us fortunes for taking the fortress, nor do we have any ideas of what actions could lead myself or yourself to the next life. You're a brilliant strategist Arthur but a slow warrior. I shall be at the front line and I shall make it to the gates whether you stand near my flanks or not, But even with your strength and your cunning Arthur none of us can predict the actions of those who have enough gold to buy the armies and mercenaries that we are in abundance."

His point was driven into the night as hard as if used a hammer to strike it in. Mazeky took a bite and pulled the flesh out of the piece of meat that oozed grease into his hand. Arthur took another sip from his metal straw and thought to himself. Their closest followers around their campfire sat in silence waiting for one or another to lighten the mood of the night as the words of Mazeky had weighted it to the ground. Both leaders had a lot to think about with the time of battle drawing closer. Both men sat, staring into their own views of history. Both men sat in silence while the fire burned on. "What kind of a name is Raykken," Mazeky said with a slight gesture. But the silence continued with no laughter. Arthur straighten his back and took another sip from the beverage in his hand. "Listen," he said while clearing his throat. "We have all been hired by the same contractors and I am sure his intentions are honourable, we will all run into the fray with no fear and celebrate a victory with more drinking and music than we have tonight. We shall be paid in gold and honour I am sure of it. Mazeky smiled at Arthur and looked down at his drink. "As long as he worships the right gods, then he will be noticed as honourable. A good amount of faith can persuade a man to pay all debts, realise his talents and bring him to do right by the people." he stood from his seat to a few claps from his warriors, gesturing with a bow. Arthur smiled clasping his drink in his hand, looking at the sudden turn from his verbal adversary. "Really" he cried out stroking his beard, "and which gods would that be?" The groups of men around the fire gazed at their leaders with anticipation, all members of both guilds had marched for days together but neither band of men had commented on the belief of gods. Generally, those who worshipped the gods of war joined guilds and from one town to another, both groups of men seemed to believe, up until this point that the other worshipped the same god of war on the battlefield.

Of all deities out in the world, the largest pantheon of gods was awarded to the deities of war. Not to say that these legendary beings were all related but generally, the idea was that the worship of one god of war was better than the others. All the gods of war also stood for emotion or agitation that was presented higher than most other emotions or ambitions. Truth, justice, conquest, freedom, ambition, furthering of the races, honour, death in premise, presenting to lovers and even atrophy. The gods of war came in more varieties than all the other gods and all had some strange adornment that placed them more nonsensical than the last and with it, their worshippers showed more signs of wild eccentricity than those who worshipped the gods of the harvests or the gods of soup. Such as those who believed in the hostile ogres of the northern caves, generally would destroy those who did not believe that the club was the superior weapon, to be used by all mortals but that It needed to be wielded with skill. Those who worshipped The Bear God of Salifice would tie blades to their fingers with string made from hair and would not fight on the days of the blood moon, as that was the sacred day dedicated to being feasted on and for its followers to wear 'the skins of the forest'. Those who worshipped the mysterious being known as Qyldis The Black Hand was said to burn their firstborn son's at the age of twelve, and from that moment on they had to be dedicated to dying on the battlefield, at the age of nineteen, if they had gathered enough immolation they would be rewarded with males and female lovers. Those who worshipped Mexlin, God of the Corpsman required that all who fell on the battlefield was to be taken care of, no fighting was to be held on the seventh day, unless in self-defence and his banner to never be held face down. Otrena, Goddess of Torture and one of the few demi-goddesses of war, required the fallen enemies of her devotees to have their hands nailed to a plinth that was presented before battle by standard-bearers. Survivors of battle were to be placed in extreme pain immediately and all who lived in the city of Noserta were required to worship her. The gods of war had been worshipped by many and while some had honourable and acceptable devotion practices and others came with strange rituals and crazed followers.

Mazkey smiled with his beard, his hand still clasping his horn goblet, while his other hand held a now empty bone. Having his idol close to his heart hidden under his gigantic leather chest guard. He normally was the more humoured of warriors with his usual actions of leading the men while keeping their spirits up. It was rare that he was engaged in serious conversation and from this, he was normally seen as a quipster and of this, his answers were of a humorous nature. Always quick to lighten moods and lead his men with personality, boosting morale while doing so. Arthur had brought out a more arduous complexion in Mazeky those days they had travelled together. Most had looked at him still as the quipster leader, that fought with his honour and which but his one eye betrayed that he was more than was presented and Arthur saw this more than anyone. "Which god do you invest your faith in?" a voice cried out from the darkness leaving a mood in the camp that the members could swear on. Mazeky raised his chest to present a big, booming voice to blow most of the embers into the sky in an unneeded theatrical attempt to set fire to the nights azure. "Why Imes of course, The God of Freedom, defender of the stricken, installer of the people, keeper of honour on the battlefield. Who else would need to be worshipped than one so powerful as he?" a cheer erupted through half the camp as men raised tankers to the sky and roared with passion.

Those who worshipped Imes, The God of Freedom, usually walked on the just side of war. Battles were to be fought with honour and dignity. Only those who allowed themselves to grace the battlefield were to be challenged and all unarmed combat was to be fought fairly. His worshippers were known to be fair to villages that had been held captive and never to mutilate women or children unless challenged to a duel. The Temples of Imes stood proud made of wood and always were well cared for, his statues graced numbers of paths, mountains and valleys with pilgrimages only consisting of battles to be fought. It is said that he was the cry of all just warriors on the earth and that those who fell in his words of honour would be carried to Dimenses, the great beer hall in the sky where they would drink with the mightiest of warriors from the past. His being came to be a god, through merit, It was said that he stood on a battleground as the last remaining warrior against an entire army. The army had ambitions on the peoples of the nearest village and it was said that Imes, armed with only his axe stood between the mass hordes of bloodthirsty wretches and the innocent villagers of women, children and the old and the sick. Unlike any normal man, Imes swung his axe straight into demons that ran at him and held them off long enough for all to escape. Taking many wounds and dripping in his blood and that of the enemy, he would not stop. Once he had driven the horde into retreat, he let his hands fall to his sides and allowed his axe and armour to fall upon the ground and he prepared himself to die in silence. But the gods of war had heard his cries while he thought the horde. They watched as with his might he took the full blows of bodies being thrown at him, Bites being left in his arms and legs, sword slices and arrows embedded in his flesh. He fell to his knees but the gods would not let his face fall to the ground. Instead so impressed by him all the gods raised him to the status of deity and allowed him his own paradise. His idols all carried the sacred axe on their chests, which was common as the worshippers wanted the axe of the hero on their chests as well.

Arthur merely sat in his chair and took his last sip from his goblet, placing it on the ground once he had finished wiping some stray drops from his beard. The forward-thinking leader of the other guild was the opposite of his fellow leader. Where Mazeky was extravagant with his diatribe, Arthur would speak to the accomplishments they could achieve. While Mazeky would talk to the hearts of his troops, Arthur would speak to their minds. Mazeky had the tactics of a noble warrior and would take action to serge with pure strength at his enemies. Arthur would be very different in this aspect. He had been known to plan out all events and find out the best way to flank and overwhelm his opponents to the point victory would be assured. His plans were wise and his soldiers were loyal because of it. Never had he marched into battle without thinking what would be the best way to win the fight and with the least of his men wounded, killed or subjugated. As the leader of his city and through his faith, Arthur was looked up to as the astute elder that he was but looked towards the future in expanding his lands and territory towards the outer lands and one day beyond the hills that blocked his view. His children sat near him, around the campfire but he kept one at home to lead his people if Arthur was to not return on one such campaign. The ambition of conquest had been in the dreams of Arthur for some time now, his prayers always contained it and his meeting of these other mercenaries conscripted into a battle that could change the world were seen as a good omen. His thoughts had consisted for the last few days of "Why not, the gods made this happen to help the understanding of the battlefield" and of course the gods could not be wrong. For the gods placed tools for victory to be achieved and up to this moment he had never been crestfallen. Arthur smiled on his one-eyed counterpart trying to hold his experienced appearance, looking on all who counted on him too. For there was only one thing that would make Arthur break his subdued demeanour.

His faith, his belief in the one god of war that had to lead him to victory and aloud to expand on not only his knowledge of victory but claim some fields and farms that once belonged to barbarians and allowed him to claim gold and status. The god to dedicate victory, reward and status too, Umes, The God of Conquest.

It was said that no amour shined greater than Umes in the fields of paradise, only those of great achievement could sit next to him at the table of titleholders. While he was not the highest-ranked member of the Parthenon of War Gods he still sat towards the right hand of the prospect and thus making him worthy to be next in order of worship. It was said that Umes once lived as many around him. Taken as a boy from a village, after the slaughter of his parents, elders and sold into slavery with many of his kin. He was raised in the private army of a wealthy merchant. The merchant used many of these laboured soldiers to protect his caravans filled with cargoes, keep trade stalls open and intimidate cities to allow him to control their bazaars. On some occasions when cities foolishly stood up to the merchant, he would send in his slave army and take the city for himself. Umes proved himself a great warrior, fearless but also apt. He commanded other troop members and rouse up the ranks, being at one point the most important member of the slave army. Time passed and the merchant's trade routes became a small dominion of port cities and trade routes. Gaining the respect and reputation to command his other troops that the slave army one night awoke with an orchestrated event and took all the merchant had in one night. Umes was placed as the leader but could see for his new dominion to continue it had to gain in size, strength, accountability and reputation. Soon he took over greater cities inland, capturing farm territories so there was no longer a need to import food and to feed all of his new citizens. He reformed, installed a voice for his people and gained the trust of all. Umes cultivated his dominion into an empire and stood fast in all his battles, not only through his fierce battle presence but also his planning of full battlefield actions, he wrote his words on scrolls, lectured his subjects on how to live and spread his teachings across the lands to better the understanding of his intension and life structures. It was said that on his deathbed, he was still gracious and all of his empires came to see him into the afterlife. The gods took notice of him and welcomed him into paradise, not as a normal soul but installed in him the powers to become a god. From that moment on he was worshipped and his temples kept in them the flame to never be extinguished for all time. His message was carved into the rocks of his temple, "You who come after me, go forth and bolster your number" which many took to mean, go forth and conquer to increase the strength in his name. The empire that he created fractured into smaller dominions and cities, while each tried their construction of going forth and bolster. But some took his worship as a blessing and would never allow the misinterpretation of his words. Arthur had his words copied on sheepskin and made one of his number carry it around with him at all times for him to learn from it and be more involved in the worship of the God of Conquest, Umes.

Both gods had their followers and both sets of followers believed that he was the true god of war and the teachings of his deity, was the true path of the warrior. One was planning and strategy, the other strength and honour. Whoever believed any different walked a strayed path between these two secs. Both leaders of the guilds kept their eyes and eye on each other. Mazeky still embracing the adulation from his troops, noticed his newly made friend was not cheering or raising to the occasions. "So you do not rise" his voice was thrown towards the fire. "Might I guess that it is not the rightful God of honour and freedom, Imes that you worship?" Arthur did not engage with his co-leader in such angst. Instead, he sat and smiled, thinking to himself what would be the best way to answer the question that had been put before him. Though as noble as both messages of both gods were, their followers had been know to take their words too much to heart. Villages had been torn to the ground in the name of war, in the name of both gods. Freedom and conquest had been forced on the peoples of this land with fewer thoughts than that had been used in the conversation that had happened but moments ago. Mazeky grew impatient with the silence that had graced the camp and started to speak with jovial remarks made of blundering restlessness. "So who could it be? Not Mexlin? No, Your words do not ring with medicine in mind, nor would I say that you have entered the cave temples of Gatnas. No those who cannot walk in the light would dare enter his worshipping grounds." He walked around the fire slowly. A dagger had been tucked into his belt sometime, used to separate tuff meat from the bone, slight trinkets hung from his leather amour and his hair had been braided for the warrior's code. He had looked around at everyone at the camp and noticed the grey silence that had greeted the camp, the embers had seemed to stop crackling on the log bark that laid in the fire. He had decided to lighten the mood. "It couldn't be Otrena because I see no severed hands around this area and you don't have any burns on your beginning so I could not be The Black Hand and you seem too valiant for it to be Umes." With the words of Mazeky falling from his mouth, the empty jests of fool hearty leader had placed on the mood, like kindling on the fires around their camp. Some of the troops moved on the uneasy knee, while others reached for weapons to be ready. Mazeky, in his brash favour, noticed a fierce change in the mood, not only of the camp but of Arthur, who up until this moment had a seriousness that weighed of only light elements. "Ohhh" the words of Arthur arouse to himself to his feet. "and what follower of the rightful god of war am I? How many valences should I lack?" He clutched the sword by his side, walking towards Mazeky, he kept his voice at mid-level but let his eyes widen in the night. "Surely it is full hearty for a man to believe that a god, who commands his followers to run into battle with no insight should be the one who has his best interests in mind? What makes a god of fools who do not plan their situations with no reason better than the supreme intelligence that has been presented to us from a God whose will is compelling." Mazeky pulling himself forwards towards Arthur. "A man who has more honour to believe that he has freedom with his faith more than the man who conquers those and forces his faith on them." The words of Mazeky followed with the stench of meed onto the face of Arthur and left his nostrils with the indignity of foul-smelling harsh words. "Fortune favours the bold sir, with every march the conqe…" Arthur placed his finger on the breastplate of Mazeky. Mazeky quickly pulled a gloved hand up from the space it had been resting and struck his former reserved worded friend with force into the dark spaces beyond the firelight. "Never lay your hands on me with your misguided efforts ever again." The tension in the camp had aggravated beyond capable and while all looked on, their unwatched hands reached for the instruments of defence scattered about the camp. "And what if I was to lay my well-directed hands on you again?" Arthur shouted over Mazeky's Skull. "Don't you dare try" Mazeky shouted back. Arthur raised the hand that had been discarded and stuck his finger out. He mockingly turned it towards him and placed his finger again on the leather breastplate of Mazeky. Mazeky looked down at the finger that had violated the space of his armour and the surface of his honour. He took a deep breath and cried out loudly towards the sky, "By the voice of Imes, may his freedom cry rain over us all!" He raised the hand he had used to strike away Arthur's hand, closed it well to form a fist and struck Arthur close to his cheek. Cries roared into the darkness as men jumped at each other, violently awakening the camp into an eruption of fighting. Those who had drunk together suddenly fought for the honours of their leaders, their homes and their gods. The night sounds had stopped filling with crickets, insects, owls and other animals that called the plains their home and instead gave way to battle that was now the night. As the sounds of men destroying each other continued into the darkness, Sebastian just sat, with his wooden guide resting on his shoulder and waited for it all to finish.

It was unbeknownst to Sebastian that the air around him had faded from the darkness of the night and the orange of campfires to the blue before dawn and it was at this time finally the last voice that moaned for some sort of solace, whether it came from their gods or their parents, finally fell silent. The cold air had greeted the morning dew, creating a mist in the air. Old Sebastian felt his bones crack as he raised his skull away from the cold morning air. The wooden staff raised off his shoulder where it was once perched and proceeded to pull him again, this time towards the battlefield. The old blind man uncrossed his legs and placed himself with much trouble on his feet. Feeling fatigued that he was now tired of, old Sebastian started to become more numb to these situations than he had been in the past. For someone on a journey that had taken him so far, for now, he was wishing it to end. These thoughts briefly appeared in his head but without the strength in his arms or knees to break the wooden staff, he just let the silent leader pull him through the fields stained with unneeded deaths of young men and walked silently through the mist hoping in his mind that those who were responsible in giving him this quest were just over the horizon.

<u>Chapter Ten:</u>

With his footsteps leading him at his measure, old Sebastian made his own progress through the mist that would hinder so many but did nothing to his judgement. His dark world had outmatched the unease of the mist and rather than let the staff pull him towards the still unknown destination, he placed one foot in front of the other and simply plodded his way into the unknown created by the morning weather. He kept his thoughts to himself and his head down, letting his scars get a look glance at the grass below. The gentleness of the grass blades had been good to his feet, which also helped the old blind man make small motions across the plain that he now made tracks in. The staff had taken him on this journey and again as he had before Sebastian started to ask questions as to what he was doing. "Must I follow this stick forever?" he thought out behind the large stitches in the former residents of his eyes. "Surely I would find my way by now?" He kept taking his steps while letting the staff guide his direction. "How long has it been?" another question entered his frame of mind. His hand still gripped to what had been his guide through all of this, guiding him from the dusty streets of the bazaar, onward past villages where people used their gods to practise bigamy, past swaps filled with the bodies of those who could not be protected from the words sorrows or it's careless wills to cast the weak out into the rain and stank of the fragile nexus of life, broken by unstoppable forces of cruel intension. Old Sebastian had witnessed the rotting emotions of greed, jealously and malignity come to grab unsuspecting travellers from their paths much walked and subjected to pestilences and robbery. While he had heard miss spoken words that stoked the fires of the hearts of young men and had felt the fury of ignorant rage rupture the physical beings of those strong young fellows. Leaving their minds fractured in the wake of their survival. All of this is in lieu to hope for an afterlife of some suggestion or a desire to be guided to the right path towards a good life. Given what Sebastian had understood he didn't want to partake in any of these wretched outcomes. The old blind man would rather have been left to his devices while living a happy life, but the process of life had prompted him to throw off the divine influences of faith and try to warn those in public from making the prodigious mistake he thought everyone had made.

He had known of the stories of the gods, he had picked them up over the years and while he begged in the alleys of the bazaars, he heard the legends that came with the floggings of wares to the public that wanted something impossible to happen. As he had lost the passion to do his former profession and was stripped of the ability, he was forced from that moment to listen, and remember the stories he had been told and learned the descriptions of the idols, talismans and mementoes that had been coveted by so many. Without his sight or his sanity, he had been punished to involve himself in the one subject he had loathed for casting him into the darkness in the first place. The calls of crows cackled into the distance, the soft mist had played games on his face. The smell of grass levelled itself into the air and would not leave him alone. While his steps continued into the opaque world around him, his thoughts still kept to themselves and rather than needing an angelic shine to guide him towards his destination, he had the company of a silent wooden friend that never guided his past but instead showed him signs of the truth he knew all along. To the blind man, for some time there appeared to be nothing around him but grass and animals taking on the compromise of the morning grovel. Nothing needed to be explained, just the natural order of life. Nothing getting in the way of the birds he heard, calling to each other or banging their beaks on the ground to source the morning breakfast. Sheep called over the mounds of grass they ate from slightly while defecating on the ground to fertilise the soil helping them continue the cycle of life. Sebastian's steps seemed not to disturb the surroundings of the plain, instead, the wildlife around him seemed to take no notice of this unthreatening miscreant. He felt so often a rabbit, brush passed his rags, the call of more sheep into the distance around him, the boy of a small frog that hid under his foot as he steps and softly covered itself in the soft green, creating a cover of protection from the lightweight of the old blind man. Even the staff made a sort of effort not to disturb nature will as the steps continued into the null. It placed itself forward over and over missing dandelions and other small flowers around its stride. Not a petal was harmed, not a stem out of place, nor a root torn from the ground. Bees kept pollinating the world around both of the pilgrims in this land and with the sounds of some insects in old Sebastian's ears, they seemed to pass him and leave him to his objective. It was as if the passing of time had lead Sebastian to be a part of the land, to march the fields without disturbing the nature of not only of the plain but also the progression of humans in history. This was the opposite to what he had done in civilisation, calling his thoughts out to passers-by, but from his surroundings, he was now learning silence.

His steps continued with his strength slowly fading into the air while leaving his body, his will had been broken and if it was not for the gentle pull from the wooden staff, he would have laid down in the field and wait for the ground to claim him for its own. Not thinking of the hunger that had gripped him, the depression that had dented his desire, the pain that sacked his body or tempest that wrecked chaos inside him. The constant wonders of denial inside of his mind, combined with his sheer force of will to oppose what he had proved with the object in his very hand. He was no longer in need of questions but instead kept to him close, the silence of the fields that encircled him. The cold gathered on him, letting his skin know that it had a presence to him, the mist entered his bones and made them hurt to the point his joints moved without being prompted. Knots appeared in his limbs and cracked, making sounds that echoed into the distance, letting the old blind man know of their effect by causing an ache in his appendages. He felt his body hang lower towards the ground and throughout the trail, from this moment on he was greeted with the prospect that he would never find out the destination of his journey, that he would be unable to continue and that he would be the end. "Falling face down in the cold soil wouldn't be so bad? Maybe the sores of my souls will finally stop hurting," he said under his breath, pulling his body across the plain, trying to keep up with the wooden staff. His shoulders kept forward, bending his back to push his weight on the staff to ease the pain he felt in his body, his request for sleep had been refused and the more the steps he took, the more the soil felt harder on his heels, the more his knees buckled under his weight, the more his head throbbed in the pain inside his eye sockets. It had been a long journey through all the lands he had crossed and now the old blind man just dreamed in a waking state. Dreamed that his journey was over, that he could lay in a bed, supported by hay and waking up to a good breakfast that he could feast on, but these were the wishes of a lazy creature, not deserving of great truths that would corrupt the minds of the unworthy. His presence now resembled an even weaker, version of himself the longer he walked into the fog. The cold that ate into his bones racked him with pain and continued to play tricks on his seams. The wounds on his body started to weep and dry below where they had seeped out, but the refusal of the wooden staff to cease the journey it was taking him on kept him walking into the unknown. "I am in need of rest if you can hear me?" he said out loud to the world hoping that his wooden friend could hear him. From this no reply was heard, the staff didn't change course or yield on its trail. Old Sebastian stumbled a few steps when his feet hit some holes hidden in the earth and bent one of his toes on a mound that caught his stumble. "Surly our travels can come to a rest at this moment?" he called out, with again no reply. The old man had been dented many times on this pilgrimage and now it had worn him thin. He no longer had bread to stuff in his mouth, he wished for a warm meal and maybe some bread to dip in a soup of boiled vegetables. His memories of warm meals had faded over the years due to starvation in alleys, begging for meals had become normal for so long that now, now he with no prospect of eating thought in his deficiency back to the times he had been welcomed to dinner tables, times when he had paid for hot pies with gold straight from his pockets, food with people he had respected and treasured their company. The old blind man had felt sadness in his heart, he no longer could shed tears. His tear ducts had been removed with the violent acts committed against him. His urges had grown monstrous inside him and now, beaten by hunger, tortured by pain, ravished by cold and strained by doubt he wished for it all to stop, but as long as his hand remained clenched around his wooden guide, the staff that lead him so far, his journey would continue. The agony that had built up inside his skull echoed into the darkest parts of his mind making a waterfall of fury pour from the vilest reaches of his mentality.

"Surely you can end this? I do not wish to continue, you have dragged me far and wide, for days, weeks, maybe a month, I am unsure but you can end this. I do not believe in you, I have no faith, I refuse, but with the littlest doubt, prove me wrong, you unnamed beasts of morality. Darkness, fear and blight were my closest allies but now they have turned on me, thrown me to your path, under a carriage that let its wheels break my resolution. I am tired" his words cried out into the murky distance of the unending horizon. "I forgot her name, was that not good enough? I had my eyes taken, was that not good enough? I have marched from the streets where I was treated as pestilence and caused harm to the middle of unseen dull fields. Have I not suffered enough?" Old Sebastian had reached the end, the end of a string that he held that kept him in the living world and now with nothing more to help his misery go away he called out to the world and received no reply in return. The natural sounds of the world were the only harmony he was given and the quiet thuds from the staff in front of him as it tapped the ground. A crack sounded in one of his joints that gave relief to his blight but still, his journey carried on. Time was no longer distinguishable to him, his darkness had eliminated the need for day and night. The temperature of the fields had been the same since he had left the wastes of the campsite behind him, some time ago. With the pulling of the staff leading him ahead, he had no choice but to slip into a habitual reflex and keep journeying the pilgrimage until it was deemed final.

Chapter Eleven:

The sounds of an instrument woke Sebastian from his nomadic al unthinking world. His steps in the fog had come back to him with sounds of grass being trampled underfoot, yet in the distance, someone was pulling chords on a stringed instrument, it made some condensed sounds and then gave the world a slight medley as the played finally built up confidence to build to a song. It made some strange pulled noises and swung them through the mist with more. It cackled like many grating moments playing at once and built up in speed with its melody and suddenly became happy in motion disturbing the lonely atmosphere in the world. Sebastian felt the cold ground but a sensation woke in his bones and being able to move his legs faster, the momentum of step quickened. Sebastian's years listened out for the direction in which it was coming from, over some delusional hills and curving to the ground under the fogs dread and escaping towards the end. The old man didn't know if turning towards mounds or puddles could help him find the source of this measure of sound but the wooden staff seemed to have a destination in mind and noticed Sebastian's return of energy. The old wooden friend pulled him along the way and Sebastian felt happiness inside him which warmed the strings of his heart. The sounds moved to their own accord and needed a solid heart to tame it, a solid heart in control with skilled hands to enchant every melody. Sebastian moved forward, further into the mist and for a while for miles he could only smell the odd remarks of mould in the air, the smell of damp resurrections from many pools of water. Some that he stepped in himself and the festering stenches from his wounds, battling infections he had gotten used to. Now, he could smell the undistinguished smell of onions and freshly found mushrooms cooking into the evening's sky. He, that is the old blind man, had not smelled cooked food since his night's stay at the Bourges village. Now the smell of cooked food and sweet music placed a warmth that he could feel inside his body and a pang of hunger which he felt in his stomach. He pushed his wooden companion forwards towards where he believed it to originated but with the action being unneeded as the staff seemed to be going towards the sounds and smells, to begin with. Sebastian placed his feet less carefully, tripping in holes every few yards and getting himself wetter with more cold grass and water spraying on him, but he ignored it instead steeping through his darkness towards the prospect of a hot meal. After a few more long strides forward his black venturing felt heard something more than just music in the air. It was singing, voices of men. Voices that sang together with slight rhythm but being out of sync. "I have a lamb, I have a lamb" the voices began again. "I have a lamb, lamb" a first voice started with the second falling slightly short on the last word. "A pretty little lamb, she is warm in the winter and pleasant in the summer but her dad doesn't like me coming round, so I miss her all the time and wait for the days of my pretty little lamb." The singing seemed more improvised than rehearsed and while the music played, one voice would carol out loud while the other would try and keep up. "Come on Harold" the voice chimed in still singing slightly. "Try to keep up" fun and laughter chuckled out, Harold shouted out in reply. "My hands are bloody full, and I am doing many at a time" the voice sounded a little strained while striking marks burst into the chorus of the instrument playing. The player halted his jib and the voice of Harold shouted into the fog. "IS ALRIGHT FOR YOU, You ain't doing nought." He was clearly agitated at something while using large amounts of breath and anger, tunnelled into his action. The striking sounds spared into the surroundings and helped Sebastian in their position. "I would help Harold" A voice replied trying to offer salvation to Harold's ill-humour, "But you said we dishonour the soup and therefore would dishonour the god. Now I agree my cooking abilities lead to just wastes of food, and but I done my bit in getting the water and Edward got the firewood, so this is all you." A sting twanged into the night as the music maker tuned slightly the instrument. "I set the fire, The least you could do is keep an eye on the water to boil, we need that for the soup base." Harold replied. "Your onions are burning," said a third voice, in a calm and even fashion. Scrambling could be heard followed by angry mumbling and slight calls of adulation, followed by the sounds of water being pouring into another pot. "First must be the base cooked well and together for flavour, that is commandment one." said Harold, "Come on Harold," said his obvious humorous friend. "It will be this time next year before we get a sip of that if you carry on." "Shut up" Harold scowled, he had been driven to the end of his fuse with unknown actions. Edward spoke up in his monotone again to the other two squabbling companions, "There is someone in the fog." "Who?" "I don't know" he replied, "They be dressed in black though." "Might it be death?" Said Harold, "Marching in his long black cloak", "No, he has a staff, death only carried scythes." "Who goes there?" Harold called. "Your soup is boiling," said Edward. Harold turned to his soup and moved the pot away from the fire, using an iron hook on its handle. His opinion was obvious that no matter who Sebastian was the soup was more important. Sebastian stopped but his staff kept moving towards the three companions, "My name is Sebastian, I am just an old blind man in need of rest and warmth from this cold weather." The three men looked at him through the mist and looked at each other. "Come sit with us noble traveller" A voice ran out, "We have plenty of space and warmth from the fire and once Harold speeds up we will have plenty to eat."

The Three men made space for Sebastian and watched him sit down without sitting in the fire itself. The old wooden staff leaned on the shoulder of Sebastian, letting the bottom end rest gently on a stone that formed a wall, protecting the surroundings from the fire and the fire from wet grass. The three men watched their guest with eyes of curiosity. This man with strange wounds moved his way out of the unseen lands and sat in front of them by means of being guided by a piece of wood. Harold went back to tending to the soup, while Edward plucked at the strings of his Instrument. It was a strange-looking thing.

The instrument itself was a type of music box that sat on the ground, it was between the sizes of medium and small but by how it looked, The music box could be carried around with ease. The instrument was made out of ruff cut pieces of wood, placed together with etched out notches that assembled together. Across the top of was several strings tied tight to the box that plucked would make a sound. Edward had in one of his hands, what looked like a shard of metal, smoothed by being grazed against a wall. His other hand glided over the strings plucking them in secession, His fingers moved into a rhythm and he was completely involved with the music box and nothing else in the world around him, He plucked the strings with the very tips of his fingers, creating the right context of rhythm, lowering his hand cross the box many times and back while using the metal shard that had been held with his other fingertips to counter the vibrations that his quick, well placed plucks jolted. He did not move from his knees as the music he played sped up and followed complex analogies of full emotions conveyed into tropes to lift the darkest of moments. The melody he played was different to the ballad that Sebastian had caught in the distance from the three men. A more upbeat expression that lorded the other three men to sit quietly and let the wares of thoughts take over, or in Harold's case, prepare more soup. With the melody picking up the strings moved to their own accord and needed a solid heart to tame the chords to do the music makers bidding, but for Edward, this seemed to be his paradise, lost in his own maturing wilderness and falling into the solitude that provided the amazing beauty that was his making. Sebastian could not admire the physical playing with his sight but all his other senses took the music with all its sound and feeling, then let the impression work their magic on his being. He had not felt this calm in a long time. Edward increased his agility with his hands and plucking and built the entire apex into a volcano. His hands moved fast light the demons of old and refused to slow. He worked over his emotions and created instant happiness with his explosive character in his playing of this song. It reacted to recreate its rhythm towards a party of sorts and disrupt the gloomy reactions to which the fog had created and then as abrupt as his increased tempo was, he slowed down and fell into a villagers march. It crept slower and slower to the ground giving an ear to the rest of the men so if they wished they could remember festivals of their youths where they may have danced with lovers of their day. It was a slow dance, a traditional dance, one that could bring young partners together, closer to the point of a rose and then as abruptly as he had slowed down the waltz picked up into a fever towards the sky like the great winds, faster and faster, with the mastery down to perfection, building and building the wave of music until in a frenzy of joy, it stepped into silence and the song finished.

The unnamed member of the group leads into an audience of clapping, cheering and straightened up from his relaxed position with intense happiness. "Bravo, Bravo" he shouted almost losing a long white pipe that he had taken long drags of smoke from. "The best one yet, I say anyway, never been indulged of skill like that for my entire life Edward" his voice, though that of a man who had reached maturity, seemed to ring with essences of adolescent, he laughed out loud filling the air with the physical incarnation of what the music box had supplied in metaphor. Harold raised his head for a second and tapped one free hand against his chest while clutching a chopped root vegetable in his other hand. "Very good Edward, always a pleasure." Edward smiled in silence while stretching his fingers and pulling his wrists, His deminer was subtle unlike his playing of the music box. He wore a green flat hat on his head with a matching waistcoat, knotted with several brown buttons and a faint blue thread that had been sewn into the collar to define the deminer of the wearer, such as so he would not be missed with his pleasant modesty. Under his green waistcoat was a white, collarless shirt made of not fine materials but comfortably threats that held their standards on his shoulders. Worn on his legs were a pair of grey farmers trousers held to his person by a brown wicker belt. His sturdy brown boots came up to his knees and had been giving a lifetime of endeavour. Still, Edward looked at his one prized position, the music box and gave it the same attention as he would give a child. Harold began muttering some words under his breath with quick notions, he closed his eyes and started to believe what he said to his response. Saying in quick mentions of ingredients. He was dressed mostly in rustic colours and wearing a large hat with a big brim, that formed into a dome above the top of his head. It was a surprise to notice that his grand hat was not slipping over the front of his eyes and making him cut his fingers while preparing the soup. He was covered in a large looking coat that pieces of string waiting to be attached in holes on the other side of the gap. It had been worn well and was coved in stress marks and gashes from what looked like untamed wilderness. His hands were covered in dirt and stained by the ingredients he lovingly attended to and once clutched onto a knife that he was using to chop and peel different vegetables. Sitting next to him was a wicker bag with a crooked handle. It sat open to the world, filled with green leafy produce, rooted plants and what looked like butter wrapped in a white paper. He rocked back and forth with his knife in his hand, head down, eyes closed asking for a blessing to be put on the soup he had been preparing. The third man leaned back slightly against his bag filled with what looked like herbs and bottles of some kind and placed a small plump hat with a short brim on the floor. His jacket as well oversized was coloured in a fairly odd way, as someone had in store, a handful of dyes and decided to rub all of them into his coat. It had greens, reds, opals, ochres and was also accompanied by a festival of stains from several originators. His clothes by far were the shabbiest, with holes around his knees, patches sown to his elbows and a few missing buttons where buttons should be. Placed in one of his hands was a pipe that he took long, thick drags from while exhaling smoke on intervals, adding to the fog that was close all around them. Smiling he finally came to his senses and spoke. "Sorry, about being for those moments there, but when he starts playing it's a sight for sore eye…" he stopped suddenly realising the words he chose were poorly selected. He looked at the blind man, his wounds, his clothes and his staff resting on his shoulder. "Do you mind if I help you?" he said kindly, "you see I be a medic, not a bad one if I do say so my self and oh god I did it again, didn't I" Sebastian kept himself still and spoke as to not make the man feel any worse than he already did. "If you can ease my wounds and help re-bandage me then it would be much appropriated." The man smiled and grabbed his bag. "I have bandages and ointments so don't be afraid. By the way, my name is William, that one over there playing the music box is Edward, And that one there praying over our evening meal is Harold. Pleased to meet ya." William pulled out some bandages and bottles from his bag that he had dragged to Sebastian's side, He took the old man's arm, placed it on his knee and soaked a cloth in a potion that he had pulled from his bag, The cleaning of his wounds stung Sebastian but being in constant pain, refused to let the heavens know of his uncomfortable position and sat silently. "Well, in the style of all things," William said, "who might you be?" His words came at a time when Edward had stopped giving the music box all his attention and at a time when Harold was rooting in his wicker bag for more ingredients. He pulled a few carrots from their resting place and started peeling. "My name is Sebastian" the old blind man simply replied. "Well now pleased to meet ya, we only have three bowls but you're welcome to use my one after I use it." William tied the bandages around Sebastian's feet, hands and placed ointment on the cuts on his face. "This will help heal it," he said "might stop the nasties get in there too". His deminer was too excited for what the situation called for. "We are the Confessors and we are on a pilgrimage to the city of Kezem, There we must split up and continue our journeys alone. Harold kept up with his prayers of the soup while presenting in one hand a peeled and chopped carrot, with his other hand holding a small cube of butter. "May the carrots always be added last with butter" he called out into the world and dropped the carrots into the put he was cooking his soup in. "Bit of a Strange one, your god is Harold" William said with a smile on his face stretching out the cloth to rap more of the blind man's wounds. "Dedicated to the endless seasoning of soup and whatnot." Harold stirred the first pot that contained the soup a few times and then pulled a cup from his side filled it from a second pot that was simmering water in it, he edged forwards, grabbed Sebastian's hand and placed the cup inside his palm to let the blind man's fingers close for him to hold a refreshing amount. "With all your judgment William, you forgot to keep our fourth member's thirst at bay," he said smiling back at both of them and heading back to the boiling pot of soup. Harold seemed, now that the pot was being looked after more calm than he had been for the minutes before Sebastian arrived. "I must confess," said Harold, "once good work has been done to try and appease he who is above us, it fills me with good repercussions, in the soup I trust." Sebastian peaked his head above his shoulders with intrigue. He had not heard of these practices before. "Does he wish to feed some sort of god or beast in some sort of heaven?" he thought quietly to himself. The blind man had his wounds sort to and drank from the cup he had been provided to loosen his thoughts from his head and allow the breath from this lungs to ask the questions he had forming. "Which of the gods do you worship Harold?" he said facing in a direction he believed him to be facing. "I have not heard of such designs for one deity." Harold stirred the soup while looking into the meal he had been curating over for the grand delusion. "I only worship one god, one is all that is needed in my salvation, and by his guidance I find my restored sensations to keep myself within the lines of life. It is through keeping my attentions close to me and watching over them closely that I am able to move forward in this life and one day be able to sit at the great table, Arcadia. Only then when I am placed in that seat in the great halls of the clouds, will I know I have followed the recipes to the letter is not only living but in taking care of those around me." He took out a creatively carved spoon from his jacket, placed it in the soup broth, raised it to his lips with some captured in the concaved surface and sipped from it. "More salt, more time" he muttered to himself and added salt from a small canister he had. "I worship Olio, The god of Soup, and his direction, to feed the world with the fair bowls of soup" His face looked up to the flame with pride letting the golden glow brace his cheeks, lifting his strange message higher to the rest of the 'Confessors' Sebastian listened to the words of satisfaction with an inquisitive nature. These words of a deity to bring such nonchalant joy in this one man's heart and for others to mock him but he never showed them hatred or indignation. He continued with his cooking with the only objective to make soup and travel to god know where. Sebastian spoke letting his words associated with the fires from that were fulling the pots to boil in the nighttime. "I have never really heard of such a god, epically one of soup." His words made their way to the ears of and with some strange movements the face of Harold radiated, brighter than the fire and he turned towards the blind man. "now you dunnit" said William. Edward started plucking at the strings of the music box again and let his notes fade over the hills into the fog of the night. The sky seemed clear slightly while these musical gems carried away into the air around them. Harold placed the spoon he was holding into the soup and cooperating with Edwards playing. Both seemed to feel the energy of spirits in their actions and while the music, playfully kept all the men grounded to the earth, Sebastian could feel something coming. Harold started speaking.

"Long ago, The earth had been created, the ingredients had all come to pass and gathered and man was yet to understand how cooking could be. Man scurried the earth, needing to be fed but yet eating only the raw ingredients around them, and man prayed on the shooting stars that fell to earth and they asked for a way to cook, to survive and to enjoy. From the star Olio was born, His spirit arose from the ground he fell to and he began running through the fields of wheat he saw first, then he saw the gathering huts of the first men, and the land they had not used to its full potential. This saddened him to know that with an earth full of abundant things, human beings had no way of getting the good out of them. So he presented the first beings with fire that he took from the sun, he had them lay down some wood in a circle and placed the fire on it, he then hollowed out a tree trunk of an old tree and placed water inside it, he then took a few branches and placed them in such a style that they held the trunk above the fire and boiled the water sitting in there. The beings brought him some of their stocked items, such as food in the form of route vegetables, herbs gathered on walked trails and honey stolen from bees. He had all of these

ingredients boiled in the trunk and carved from the
discard bark bowls for the people to eat and drink
from, from the twigs of the tree he carved spoons.
Soon the villages asked him to do this every night and
Olio got tired of it. He taught the village elders how
to make fires from cracking stones together, how to
craft the holy spoons, used to stir the soup while
cooking, how to gather certain items, and most
importantly how to brew the soup. Time passed and
the beings grew careless and with less need to Olio.
The beings made their soup, but they had not realised
that when Olio made soup it gave them the feeling of
life, they never became ill and their happiness was
curtailing. Soon they became sad, unable to function
to the best that they had been before and they aged
again. Olio was sad to see this. He felt completely sad
that the beings had grown careless but it was not his
fault, it is just how we are."

Harold shuffled back towards his soup, caught up in
the story he had moved away from his put and
hearing the broth boil he went back, placed his spoon
in the soup and took a sip. "Hmm" the noise he made
was a symbol of contentment with his cooked jumble
and rejoiced for a few sends while pouring it into
three bowls he had placed on the grass. "It is said that
Olio hid from us, somewhere in the middle of the
earth, there he waits for the one that will show a care
for the craft of soup-making," he said while gently

handing two bowls of soup to William. William placed one bowl in Old Sebastian's hand and lowered it to his crossed leg to help the bowl balanced on his leg. Sebastian felt around the edge of the bowl for a spoon and found it with a few fumbles without getting soup on his now cleaner hands. "Edward?" Harold Offered the third bowl to Edward with an outstretched arm. "You eat first, I can after tune the music box". Harold struggled, took a spoon full of soup and slurped down a mouthful with a cube of potato. "If that one is able to grace Olio with a mastery of soup, The showing of care to all the ingredients used, the right sequence of adding. Then the soup of life will be awarded to he who makes the soup closest to the original Olio made. Then he will be awarded the knowledge of everlasting life and the curing of hunger and unwellness of others" He continued "Through that, through it all, no man or woman will have to suffer from hunger again, everyone will be fed." Both William and Edward continued themselves with acts to keep them occupied, William eating and Edward tuning, but Sebastian wondered in awe of the faith this man had for something that sounded hard to grasp. "Did he believe this to be the truth? The legend sound exceedingly curious." he thought to himself. For moments after those words. The men sank to silence, with only the sounds of chewing from, Harold and William, while Edward tuned the music box.

Sebastian used the spoon that was in his free hand to scoop up a serving of soup and placed it in his mouth. It was tasty from being cooked very well and the fact that Sebastian had not eaten anything warm and nourishing for the last few days. It warmed him as it slid down his gullet into his stomach and made his body feel the acceptance of comfort from within. He took another bite out of what he felt to be a potato on his spoon and soon was more encouraged by his three new companions. Soon the He had found ease in his frame and listened in on the tuning of the music player. "And what of you Edward, do you worship the gods of music or melody, The Goddess of festivals?" He said hoping his words would greet the music maker in a kind opinion. The tuning stopped and Edward placed his fingers on top of the music box. "That would make sense I assume," he said with his quiet deminer. "But alas, I do not worship any gods but more those who keep from ending in collapse." He plucked a string a few times, getting ready to follow through into another ballad of what was his journey and why he must take it. "Have you ever heard of Lakrama Mountains?" Old Sebastian had never heard of this destination before. It had not been mentioned to himself or to his knowledge those of whom he would rest near, trying to sell wares.

"I am on a pilgrimage, not to visit a temple of a god, or to find their resting place but beings created by the gods with so much promise," Edward said while starting to play some composition on his music box. "The truth is, I have never been to my destination but we need to find my way and I still have many days until I reach my destination. You see I belong to a village where they send one of their own on this pilgrimage once a year. The chosen one must march to a spot that takes many months to get to, most of the year. He will have no knowledge of the ones who travelled before until he comes across him on the way back, some never made it back but all reach the destination. All save the world." His words puzzled Sebastian, two out of three of his new friends so far had puzzled him with their faiths and beliefs. Edward kept plucking away at the music box while building the mood into the air from his nimble fingers on the string.

"Long ago, The world was created but needed to be maintained. Those who created it were not perfect and in tale neither was their creation, the earth. It needed to be maintained which the gods could not keep up with and as the waves of the oceans crashed on the shores, devouring lands, or winds that would swallow up entire forests. The gods themselves found they had been terrible at keeping their new world from harm But one of them decide to create another being to look after the world while the gods could do more meaningful things. And it was so. The gods created The Golems, great creatures, some only five cubits tall, while others towered about the trees said to be thirteen cubits. The Golems helped maintain the earth and keep clear lands, that needed to be fertilized, widen rivers to help from the lands becoming lakes, they worked hard and watched the earth mature. Animals came out of the seas and began to walk on four then two legs, but The Golems remained the same, they began to become complacent with their existences after fixing most of the world to a content fashion. They wanted to explore, create their own worlds and build ladders to the stars, but this would never happen."

Edward felt a string in his music box wane and pulled on a small rod on the side of the device to tighten the strings, he plucked it a couple of times, with each pluck he listened to every vibration the string produced. He had stopped suddenly in the middle of his story to fix his prised instrument, become silent to tend to its needs. He tapped a sting with the pick he had to pluck the instrument and then when it became apparent that he had fixed the problem, he gave off a subtle smile and dropped his breath below him. He had his head lowered, looking upon his music box, the wood that provided such stability in his life, with such love and attention that those who could see his expression could be gauged what was being thought inside his head. He breathed in again, exhaled and continued the legend from where he had stopped without missing a beat and a second later re-continued his playing.

"The gods in all their laziness failed to build a good structure above the heads that laid under it. The danger became more and more evident with every setting of the sun. One day the sky will fall. The Golems with all their wisdom found the largest mountain in the lands, the mountain that touches the sky, Mt Sadaka. There they climbed it to the peak of the mountain and steadied the summit. There they made a design of something that would outshine most of what the gods had created. They started to build onto the mountain The Great Behemoth. A gigantic creature, taller than anything living on earth with the strength superior to any being who walks today. It took the Golems so long to build him to hold up the sky, that one by one the Golems shut down and stopped moving, all but one, the last one. He struck the spark that awoke The Great Behemoth, but alas it was not the greatest of plans, The Great Behemoth was wild and though kept the sky from falling, instead wanted to bring it crashing into the earth. The last Golem made a music box similar to the one I am playing right now, he placed a song to put The Great Behemoth to sleep. Now every year, one of my people the one who masters this music box must make the great pilgrimage every year and play the melodies played by the last Golem to keep the behemoth asleep and in his slumber the sky will not fall on us, ending the beauty that is the earth. It cannot be the same player every year, the journey is too long so maybe I will meet last years pilgrim on my way there. It is an honour to play to keep The Great Behemoth in his slumber. I just hope I can keep the sky from falling."

Sebastian sat listening at the campfire to the words of Edward, to him the first two Confessors had ridiculous taste in worship. The faiths were ludicrous, Gods were childish creations of the human mind as it was, long-forgotten origin tales used to explain the worlds but these two had faiths that had lost their ways completely and spoke out loud about tales that were to do in the world with no real guidance. "There is no logic in any of their thoughts," Sebastian thought to himself quietly. He could not see the reason as to why they had chosen these faiths to follow and saw many holes in the legends. Still, both men had kinder beliefs than those who worshipped most gods. One wished to make soup, while the other was to play the music that he was admirable at to a giant mountain. Sebastian felt slightly paused in his thoughts, the old blind man didn't want to despite the kindness he had received from the three Confessors and instead of letting his feelings be known, he simply sipped the soup out of the bowl that rested in his lap. Edward placed the music box carefully to the side of his where he was sitting, looked toward Harold he had finished his portion of soup and tipped his head to the symbol he was hungry. The soup maker poured further his spoon in the bot boiling water and scooped up a few helpings of hot soup into the bowl. It steamed into the air around them from the nourishing heat. Harold placed the spoon in the bowl under a slice of carrot to help weigh it under the surface and handed it gently to Edward. The bowl had inside it a brown liquid, filled with vegetables and dotted with small mounts of flavours that refused to be submerged. Edward closed his eyes, said a prayer, raised the spoon from its murky depth and sipped with caution a mouthful of the meal he had been given. William placed a new amount of Tobacco in his pipe and stuck a long piece of grass he plucked from the ground near the fire in the chamber. He leaned close to the fire, letting the flames like the piece of grass like a green fuse and returned to the spot he had been occupying when Sebastian approached. These three men had shown Sebastian more kindness than anyone had in the latest years of the old man's life. These three Confessors did not care who he was but instead extended kindness to a fellow wanderer in the befogged cloud world. William, Edward and Harold stared into the dancing blaze. The three men were very content with their choices in life and instead of complaining about the cold or the darkness of their situations they made soup, played music and smoked pipes.

William rested his head on a mound below his back and took a deep breath of his pipe, he spewed out a couple of puffs of smoke, adding to the opiate unknown that had surrounded them and which was being kept at bay by the fire. Sebastian had finished his soup as much as he could while scooping up the failed escape pieces of food in the bowl. He placed the spoon in the almost empty bowl and held it out in front of him with his left hand. "Thank you," he said to the cook, who reached forward and took the bowl from his possession. "No mentions" Harold replied happily that he had continued the good fortune his god allowed. He looked into the soup pot, took the spoon from the now semi-empty bowl and washed it slightly in the water pot. He took a second portion of soup and filled the bowl to the top with it, Hungry he placed the spoon in his mouth, burning the roof of it while being reminded that it was still hot. His cry of pain had been kept in his mouth, as to not lose any of the sacred broth he had collected. He swallowed, "William," he said when he grained his voice from the burn, "Tell our guest who you follow. I and Edward have laid our faiths out bare, it is only fair you do too." William raised himself to his elbows and looked at his fellow companions. "Is nothing too fancy who I follow." replied musingly with a smile on his face, "Surly, he can guess from just from the actions I undertook with him?" William took another puff from his long white pip and blew it into the sky. "It is quite obvious that I am not a soldier and we doctors only follow one goddess" Sebastian raised his head, quickly, towards where he could predict the medical Confessor, he spoke out loud, which had been he had not done much of so far in their meeting. "Enva, Goddess of Healing, helper of the sick, provider to the injured, we follower her to help those who have been hurt, no matter who has fallen, bruised or abused, Her ever guided virtue will heal us all." The three Confessors stared at Sebastian in silence. His words came out as someone who had been wounded, not just by his obvious physical injures, but a deep unseen scar on the soul.

"She was born from the cry of those who needed help, those dying from diseases or injury that couldn't be cured, the infections that calmed the bodies of the young, sores that became visually raw, opened up with rotting carnage, flowing with poisoned blood. Plagues that would leave the lucky with limbs falling to the floors, and teeth turning to dust while the cries of children unable to understand their plight that they had been cursed with upon this world. The coughing of from infliction, deep in the withered lungs of barley living husks dragging themselves past suffering towards the emptiness that was death. The great plague that was formed was thrown upon the people with no sign of redemption for the poor soul's insight, The hoods warn covered the faces of grieving mothers who had to bury their children, long before it should have been necessary. The people could only suffer, watch and experience the pain of diseases, infection, loss and the end coming towards them. The great dark plagues came, falling into the towns and villages first with only the fogs symbolising the arrival of the great death. The sunlight seemed at that time to only bring agitation to the infected peoples of these areas. The heat from the summer made it worse, as the foul stench of composing wounds brought with them more infections that signalled the great pain to come. The cities started seeing people flooding into their walls, filling up all available space. Crowded streets filled with the bad touches of humour in the air that lead to more people getting sick, more people dying in the streets and more bodies poisoning the world around. They say the plague lasted so many days the people forgot the before times. The cries of the sick could be heard, the cries of dying children sounded over the walls of every dwelling in the land. All hope was lost and the end had been accepted by many. It was only in that time of need, in that period of no hope, she arrived in the capital of the region. She walked through the streets. Hair, long flowing and golden, dressed in the white and mauve colours of healing we know today. She wore her hood down to make sure the view was unobstructed to gaze at the infamy of the lands around. He quickly gave cures to those who were the most healthy, from the nectar of the Azul Plant. They grew strong and she ordered them to help the rest, she told them to go forth and cure those in need and cure the sick and weak. Weeks passed and the people became healthy again, and in one town the people took it upon their selves to raise a temple in her name. She thought many, how to dress wounds, how to create medicines, how to stunt decease. Soon Enva was seen as a saint and artists made icons in her image. Time passed and she disappeared, ascended to paradise some say, then it was said she was granted a table with the gods, then it was said she had become a goddess. Enva, The Goddess of Healing. Burn incense into the air, ring three bells above the sacred Azul Plant and pray for her to come and save the sick children. She will use her kindness to help all and fight evils that perish the body."

Chapter Twelve:

The three Confessors looked in silence at the old blind man, he had in his own way, told the story of Enva, The Goddess of Healing but without the joy and praise that they had been accustomed to from it coming from the lips of William. "Yes, I know her well," he said with his voice full of sadness. "I used to worship her." "Used too?" Said William "However could you mean? You stopped?" the fog was greeted with silence, the cold graced those not close enough to the fire, but a calm silence surrounded the flames before Sebastian gave his answer. "Yes". His reply was brief, holding in the pain he refused to let carry on his voice. William raised fully to his knees, "But why? She is the goddess of healing. She turns the sick to the well. I know her story as well. It was taught to me as a youngling, she brings all peace in life, relief in sickness..." his words were cut short but a bitter response from the fragile blind man. "Don't relay the words spoke of the goddess to me, I have heard them all over and I practised them. I heard the sermons, the prayers." The three men went back to their silent answer as they gathered their thoughts on what the old blind man was saying. His words had rattled them from the surprise of this nature. No one had spoken of the goddess in this way. Old Sebastian raised his head slightly as to suggest he was reliving a memory more pleasant than the ones he had been living recently.

"I was younger, I escaped the restraints of my origins, moved past the tragedies and lived the happy existence. That, I was told, was the only need in the world. I found myself with a wife, we met at the temple dedicated to Enva, and we fell madly in love. She and I lived our lives in pure harmony, I had a position in the temple as decant and helped the priests with their ceremonies, collect their alms of food from their walks, I helped lay down the wreaths of celebration that contained the Azul Plant, the sacred flower that cured the worst plagues. Soon, my wife was with child. She brimmed with the chance to become a mother, forever providing the necessary needs a newborn could request from coming into the world. I built what I could, I supplied what I could for the coming of the new child and she was a girl. Ethnie, named her Ethnie, a beautiful daughter. I would travel the world for her, to keep her safe, to keep her from shame and fear. My only sanctum in life was to keep her happy. She grew up strong and inquisitive, asking questions and learning. She was intelligent. My wife provided her with all the love a daughter could need, while I gave her all the attention I could muster, nothing could make me happier than having her, my Sunflower in my life. Well, the gods decided, in their wisdom that she needed to prove herself in this world. She became sick with fever, pocks, coughing fits of blood and hallucinations, she cried out to the world for it to stop, begged me to take it away. I gave her nectars that were provided by the priests, I bound her wounds that appeared on her fragile skin, I made ointments from where ever I could find the ingredients, combined with all the knowledge that I had. She was only in her seventh year and yet it was deemed by the gods that she was to have this plague on her. That she needed to prove her devotion to healing from a disease that stole the energy from her and left her brittle. I prayed, I asked if I was to be tested if I had done anything that made me deserving. I begged, pleaded to the heavens, to Enva, asked her to take me instead, tried to bargain for a cure, but nothing came. My Sunflower was left with nothing in her, and on her final day, she still looked at me, while I held her in my arms and wished only to be well again, quietly. She had left in my arms, small, thin and so light, like the feather of a bird. She was not allowed the decency of a resting place in the cemetery near the temple but instead had to be lowered into the mass graves provided for the plague suffers. I asked the priests, Why? Why could this have happened? I prayed I gave all I could to get the sacred potions, weighted on the priests so they could make prayers of her to survive and for all it was, she was taken from us. How could a goddess so divine let this happen? How could she? She is all-knowing and powerful. She had cured the plagues before and watched over us all and yet when it returned so many children had to be rolled into a giant pit outside the city. How could a Goddess allow this? How could any deity let this happen? I had lost my faith, and in that I realised, there could not be any gods, it was all conjured from stories told over and over, there are no gods. I found drink, I stopped going to the temple, I stopped my prayers. My wife could not handle what I had become. I arrived home one day drunk and she had left. I had become just the reminder of bad news but instead of improving on what my life had become, I started standing on corners and talking out loud, too loud. I wanted everyone to know the scam that had been placed over our eyes, the fakery placed on us all. Soon my words attracted unwanted attention. It started with rotten vegetables and fruit being thrown at me, then stale bread. After a short time, the bread became stones, but I numbed the pain with drink and the belief that there was no God above me, no inferno I would be cast to for spouting the words I had thrown to the people. One day while I walked through the streets I was approached by three men I once called my friends. They had grown furious with my new arrangement of belief and ordered me to stop with the nonsense and reapply my faith in the gods. I refused and mocked them for being blind to the world around them, so instead, they made me blind, violently. Those who I called my friends cut around my eye sockets with pieces of glass and tools and pulled my oculars from my head. They left me forever in the dark, but I did not die, I refused. After the holes in my head were crudely sewed shut I went back to calling my ideals on the earth. Over time my rantings became nonsensical. It appeared that the more insane I seemed the less violence came towards my direction, though I still received spit, stones or blows from physical contact from time to time. I didn't believe for so long, years of my life spent in darkness. Yet now I have been selected for a pilgrimage, I still think of it as some kind of trick, but I have been on it for some time now, I am starting to believe that no human being could keep up a charade this long."

He lowered his head, hanging it over his knees for a second, then brought it back up with his wooden friend still resting on his shoulder. His stress had flowed over the fire and burned into the night's sky, with everything he had experienced it had been a long time since someone had truly listened to him speak about his life. The old blind man had left in his emotional wake a change that the three Confessors were not expecting at the time they invited him to rest with them, eat and enjoy the warmth of the fire. The hermetic cold that hanged in the air, crept into the small camp the men had made and with only the sounds contrived from the fire and boiling fluids, an intense atmosphere appeared to hold in the awe they all experienced. William stood up from his seated position and walked over to the now crumpled Sebastian. The footsteps of the doctor could be heard in Sebastian's ears and with an instance, a silent panic ensued, this pilgrimage that he had been forcibly taken on had left him close to losing his life multiple times but now he thought that he had finally come to its end. These three men had given him kindness and in return his spat on one of their faiths in an ungrateful manner. Usually, his care for the thoughts of others had not come across his mind but with these three men, the music, the soup, the care. He felt ashamed at telling them of his past with only the murmuring of one name. To be understood in this world was hard for those who considered themselves godless and the numbers of them had become so few that Sebastian was the only one he had come across. The footsteps of William grew closer and closer with the grass under his impressions giving crunching sounds as crisp field fell to every step. Sebastian felt his presents grow closer in the few seconds it took him to arrive beside the blind old man, he brassed himself in silence, stiffening his body to receive some sort of hard blow to his body, reading himself he thought, "This is it" while knowing that, even armed with his wooden friend he could not defend himself reasonably against three men with full sight. He raised the wooden staff off his shoulder with his one hand but was too late as William was placed himself beside the knee of old Sebastian. The old man tightened all his limbs and braced, in wait for the impact of the first blow. William made some sounds while looking through his pocket and pulled out a piece of cloth to wipe a small stream of blood, from a cut that had opened on the blind man's withered head, he wiped gently and then applied pressure to hold what was left inside the head of the man that had now bared his troubles to the world. The kindness from William still had been shown in his actions which had brought Sebastian to a new emotion, sorrow. He had almost wished that some sort of violent acts would have been held against him, for that he was prepared, but instead, after knowing that he had renounced his faith, an act worst than any crime in the eyes of many, he had received kindness from this stranger and he was not prepared for it. If he was still capable he would have let tears fall down his scarred cheeks, but unfortunately, that action had been taken from him, so he instead stayed in silence. William helped stop the bleeding from the old blind man, while Harold took hold of the bowl Sebastian had been eating out of and filled it with another serving of soup. The bowl steamed into the air with its nourishing aroma. Edward looked on, watched the kindness being levied onto the old man and his reaction as to not have reserved it in such a long period of time. He stretched out his fingers, grabbed the pick he had set beside him to eat his soup and played a soothing melody that to lighten the mood around them and heal the soul of the old blind man. Sebastian felt an arm hold him close. The warmth from William kept the old man still and let his emotions raise from him without succumbing to the viscousness of the fire in front of them. The Confessors kept him in good stead but Sebastian himself could not understand why they could take time out of their important pilgrimages to make sure an old man was well in this world? Why would they not cast him out from the camp and not risk anger from their fellow worshippers or the gods they all respectfully believed in. "Why would you help me?" Old Sebastian asked them all, "Why to show me this kindness". William spoke, "My faith teaches me to look after the sick, heal the wounded, that goes for all, physically, mentally and spiritually, no matter the concession, no matter if you're a goner." Harold placed the bowl of hot soup next to Sebastian, "Here it is," he said, "about a coupla inches to ya left, you don't need to feel that pain any more, a good soup can build up strength and warm the soul". The Confessors, all three of them did not cast judgement on the old man but instead did what they felt was right to keep him on his way. William wiped down the last of Sebastian's leaking wounds and stated "We have not beer or spirits but we do have water and soup. So we shall share with as much of this as we can." Their voices echoed into the fog and without any hesitation, William headed over to the space he had been sitting in and grabbed the bowl he had been eating out of. "More please," he said chipper, with the bowl on the end of his arm outstretched. Harold took the bowl from him and filled it up and then placed it back in the outstretched hand of William. "Edward" William called out, Edward stopped playing the music box, "Could you play my girl Mary? I've not heard that one since we passed the tree lines." Edward placed his head down and tuned two of the strings on the music box tighter, he laid his hands on the strings with the pick in his right and started plucking away. "I lived in big old cities" William sang slightly out of tune to the song, "and I have lived in pleasant towns, but I never been so happy then when I was in my home. It is not from lack of company that I must confess but there has never been a girl like my girl Mary." his words twined around the notes of Edward's playing of the music box without Edward raising his head from the deep concentration he owed to his instrument.

"Oh she has a heart, a lifetime of old laughs, we never spoke ill of our futures, and even know, I left to find some fortunes, I always remember my girl Mary. Everybody now"

Harold and William song arms liked each other while William protected the soup from falling to the ground, They moved against the fire allowing their silhouettes to grace the fog behind them. They moved

their legs to act out a jig, while Edward played trying
not to get distracted by both of his friends bumping
their words into each other. Sebastian listened to the
men sing into the night's sky while reaching next to
him and placing the bowl of soup in his lap. These
three men kept their tenor high and their moral ideas
from turning their actions to hate or violence.
Sebastian breathed a sigh into the air and swallowed
another spoonful of soup. He had decided not to tell
them out the voices, or the fact that his wooden friend
was guiding him on his pilgrimage to a destination he
did not know of. So instead he listened to the gestures
of The Confessors and kept himself from making
more of a burden out of himself than he already had.
The men sang into the night while Sebastian listened
and they spoke of their journey together, All three
men had agreed at the beginning of their travel that
they would have to split up at some point, but that
would be when they reached the impasse that they
could not go to one destination without completely
missing one of the other men's destinations. They had
been walking in the fog for some time now and could
not remember when it had begun or what kind of
weather they had just before it had started. Their cares
however were found lacking and they would have
rather speak of times they ate soup and drank water
and other times they had ate soup and drank water.
Sebastian sat with them, deep into the night. William
spoke of the plans that the three men had. "We be

heading in the direction that ya came from unfortunately and we will be going early but we can leave ya some supplies in ya bag if ya like?" Sebastian spoke in the direction he could hear Harold's voice "I don't want to take your needed supplies but if you can spare something I would be most grateful." He pulled that bag from his shoulder, where it had been resting and placed it on the ground next to him. "We have plenty and can spare some" Harold said filling another bowl with soup. The singing and feasting continued until old Sebastian's head grew heavy and while listening to the gentle playing of Edward and the music box, let his head hand from his shoulders and fell asleep where he sat.

Chapter Thirteen:

The morning came slowly in the land, letting the mists of the land grow thicker as the fields grew wet with morning dew, The warm glowing embers from the night's campfire had gone to rest, and instead left behind a long black trail of smoke and the bones of charcoal turned to ash. The world started to accept The old blind man as one of its own and seemed to cover him in not only the fog of the morning but water droplets, blades of grass that had been blown over him and for a longer time moss would have grown on his being. With deep breaths, he lightly made signs that the sleep he had long entered was drawing to its final actions and with the fire no longer burning bright and warming his body, the cold finally started filling his bones again. Sebastian startled himself with a shiver from being unable to keep himself warm in the sunrise and started feeling parts of his aching limbs with his hand. The wooden staff had a small layer of frost build upon it and stood static to the elements in the air. Sebastian tried to move his hand from the staff but it was still in its parallelized state, white-knuckled while fastened to his unspeaking guide through the world. His shivers moved him to rise to his feet but before he could move one ankle he cracked several bones that caused him a large amount of pain. "Fornicating bastard harpies of whatever gods believed in by the people who cause me" he called out to the world, feeling the tearing of muscles under his skin and coughing harshly like a wild dog after his last word. "I defecate in your milk." His words came with the pain that had interrupted the healing of his mind, and yet as he listened for the Confessors he realised they had been true to their words leaving him alone again with his thoughts. His hand felt around next to him and with a few strokes of the ground, he found the bag he had claimed as his own. While moving his fingers inside to find what he had been left or what had been removed from his possession, he discovered that the Confessor had been true to their words and left a few apples, bandages and boiled water stored in a bottle for him. While his hands graced over the inner linings of the fabric the lined every stick he found a corner of sweet bread that he had thought was finished. Placing the last piece in his mouth, he chewed on it with a weakened state but allowed the pain to infect him slightly more. What else would he have in this world but pain, and misery. This divine practical joke of a quest he was on, refused to bring him closer to any answers but instead mount up his sorrows in pain, exhaustion and add woes to his being. His feet had mounted wounds added to the fatigue of his being, still, he waited for the staff to pull him forwards, for it to take him to the next destination and end his trails with some sort of closure on the matters. Just an answer might have sufficed, The stories of gods never came out and spoke to some poor soul directly. Humans were playthings of the gods and made to trace themselves towards the ends of some mystical answer. No answer was to come easy, usually, it was only the men who had lost parts of their minds that would state a god or goddess would speak to them directly and command them to build some ark or temple in the name of said deity. Weirder kings and emperors commanded on stranger days that hostile festivals had to be celebrated with mass drinking, orgies and partial fights to the death, the following to these gods never really spread past the kingdoms that had been forced to worship them and many had been stomped out of preachers mouths and confined to the ash heaps of history. Anarchy had never really been desired by communities of over a thousand devoted souls and grand ceremonies covered in the blood of sacrifice or the taking of bodies in front of fireplaces, lost their appeal when stability failed to appear. Religion was supposed to bring comfort, peace and guidance in general to its believers. Sebastian could name quite a few false teachers in his time, hearing them come to preach from where ever he had called home at the time. A few he had even saved from slash marks and general beatings that could happen if faith was deemed unworthy or worse either fake.

Old Sebastian stood for a second, placing his spare hand on his face and slapping himself gently to return to his mind to the world of the conscious. His mood was still gritty with his wounds, returning to a state of pain. The staff seemed to be allowing him to pull himself together before beginning their journey. He placed his hand in the bag that now hung across his back and pulled it towards his hip and retrieved the bottle of purified water to quench his thirst. While drinking, he allowed a small flow of water to slide from his mouth towards the rags and lastly splash on his feet. Once finished he placed the bottle back in the bag and stood in his darkness for a few seconds before uttering a word. "Let's be going then," he said to the piece of wood clenched in his hand. "Come now, take me to our next destination". The staff seemed to wait a few more seconds making up its mind whether to pull the blind elderly pilgrim to their determined destination. This struck out in one step and then a second later another and then picked up speed to pull the tired blind man towards their next journey.

While feeling the fog graze his face, Sebastian let his thoughts build inside the darkness of this head. His feet plodded along and again he became numb to the outside world to try and bear with the long directions he must take. He had stopped thinking about the destination of himself and his wooden guide. The sensations in his body came to him with fiery awareness, like he was constantly stepping on thorns from a bramble bush. His hand had entered into a constant state of cramp as his knuckles split the skin, clasped around his wooden friend. The bandages around parts of his limbs had protected him slightly from the elements but with the humidity in the air, the outer layer had taken on slight wetness and increased in mousier as the day went on. Old Sebastian had thought about the hours of the day while he walked, he no longer needed them. Daytime could be distinguished from the night and he had no engagements that he needed to keep time for. His thoughts surrounded his mind and continued to hold his attention as the wooden guide kept him on the right path. His thoughts built into his mind, words he could say to ears unable to hear him. "Annabelle I miss you, I swore I would never utter your name to anyone living, and until my death, your name will never leave my head". The words echoed in his head, leaving him unable to experience anything else. The echo had left him blind to the world and without the pulling of the wooden staff, his actions to the earth would be left quite static. While the wide-open space of the lands around him seemed to have no obstetrical except the uneven terrain of the fields below him, his mind had left in a feeling of claustrophobia. Closing darkness inside his psyche with thoughts to actions directed against him by those closes to him, by those he loved and by the gods he was told to trust and worship from an early age. His jaw refused him to speak out loud, no words could make it past the clenched grip that was made between his teeth. His tongue had rolled inside his mouth held fast by the baring of pain that had overcome old Sebastian. He wondering though the lands covered in a fog unable to be commented on.

He had not much future in his life before the appearance of the wooden staff and the golden voice inside that graced his ears. Drinking when he could lay his hands on alcohol to numb the pain. On most nights when had been unable to procure food and was refused refuge from those who it was commanded by doctrines to look after. His sickness was not to be helped, the wounds of his flesh were not to be treated, his hunger was not to be diminished and his thirst was not to be quenched. All from fear, fear that the words old Sebastian could utter would be against their gods or mythic spectres. He had stopped fearing death, the one constant he had been acquainted with for his entire life's journey. Wearing a long black cloth that had been torn in so many ways from his journeys, the smell left giant sways in the reality behind him. Being pulled along by a staff with a mind of his own. These moments he had been in touch with, the vision of what he was wearing was close to the spectre he had been told about when speaking to many about the passing to the great beyond. Tales of an old man, withered to almost nothing, carrying with him a lantern to light the ways of the dead, from this plain to the next. No matter of the will of the person, wicked or good-hearted, rich or poor, old or young, the old man of death would come for them. He could not be reasoned with, bargained with or fought, only the ending of life was his highest concern and getting the moral soul to its final place of existence. Many tales had been told of the old Spectre throwing souls into a large cage, having them locked together, grating under the power of his will. To feed the world and regrow the world items that had withered. Others believed he was leading all to paradise, where judging by the sins committed by the barer on earth, they would have to wait until their entry could be sanctioned.

If old Sebastian had his sight, the vision of his self demeanour and his appearance, akin to the old spectre would not be lost on himself, instead, he would laugh and continue his quest looking like the last image to the eyes of many. He could only at his state of being, manage to think to himself, all the wrongs that had been committed on his person and the pain that had been directed towards him after he announced his realisation that there was no gods or goddesses guiding the world. Still, with his footsteps, he felt the uneven earth under every motion his crippled hooves took putting pressure on his body with more and more falls into small mounds that clicked his already crumbling knees. He was tired, taken over with pain, impaled in his mind and unconvinced as to what was his purpose in life and yet, The wooden staff still dragged him towards an unknown direction, pulling his fragile, withered arm forwards making sure he was still moving forward. Allowing his shoulder to grind it already warn down joints almost to the point of dust. Seizing his body with the exhaustion to the point of all his body becoming a raw, arthritic state. The old blind man started to fall behind with his exhaustion but still, the wooden guide pulled him along, refusing to allow the aged shell of the flesh a chance to rest. The silent object just pressed into the ground and pushed off itself with the unseen force pulling along its venerable companion. It would not answer any questions, nor would it respond to any bargaining. It would only be responding to its mission from the unknown voice that invaded the old blind man's mind. It pulled him closer and closer, across grasslands with dips that made its old companion stumble and reach to re-establish his footing. Dragging the barer through puddles of water, murky with silt and filled with the odd fog that would be disturbed by an unsuspected foot that would fall into the water. The journey made by the wooden guide would go over hard stones that would displace Sebastian's bandages, graze the skin and reopen old wounds. It took him over logs of trees that had fallen in the fields through old age or being struck by lightning, leaving splinters in his feet as he was led to walk, uneasily over these obstacles. On and on old Sebastian was dragged through the thick fog, into the null of despair. On and on with no answers, disturbing the environment all around them. On and on he was dragged not being allowed to sleep, rest, take sips from his bottle of water. Not being allowed to stop for a bite of apples left for him by the Confessors. Through the mist, they continued. The old man was dragged with nothing more to give, his spirit was about to break with nothing more inside him but the ill-temper of a tired blind old man, tired of the wooden staff dragging him about for the acts of a journey he never wanted to go on, but the staff ignored him, he ignored his grumbling, he continued across grassed lands, across rocks and pebbles in the grounds and through streams, puddles, holes and mounds that left the old man in pain, across it all. Going and going, further towards the blackness of nothing, further towards the unrealised anguish of the unknown. It tapped the ground again and again as it advanced closer and closer to the destination of both of them, the final piece, the answer to all that the pilgrimage gad become. It continued placing itself hard into the ground, right until it lifted itself into the air and then implanted itself solidly into the ground. It stopped moving, it stopped pulling the old man. It rested where it had presented itself, and allowed old

Sebastian to reach into his bag finally and pull out the bottle of water to quench his thirst.

Chapter Fourteen

The wooden staff had implanted itself straight into the ground, becoming an immovable object that refused to continue in any direction to signal its final position. It had changed completely to what it had been while crossing the fog-covered fields, climbing the hills and mounds before the forests and passing the marshlands. Sebastian had been locked in an immortal grip with his wooden friend and now that the guide had stopped with no intention to move anymore he had become curious. The old blind man was still thankful to have full use of his hand again and to be allowed to rest after being dragged through the long valleys of grassy confusion. His darkness stopped him from seeing all that was around him, his arms were out of reach of most elements around him apart from the damp that hung in the air and his wooden guide that had stopped moving. "Why have you stopped?" Sebastian cried out to the empty world around him, he had questioned the silent item while it had dragged his tired body around the lands they had travelled and received no answers, here seemed for that moment to have the same emptiness that had come to be expected. Sebastian had no idea where he was, nor the climax of his quest. He had been dragged unpleasantly by a supposed guide for the gods, to view some repeated magnum opus of human lives to view different worship habits dedicated to random gods. Gods he did not believe in, gods he did not pray to, nor did her wish to carry favour with. It had been lost on him why he had to experience such human misery. Why he of all people had to experience more degradation than he already knew of. The fighting, the stupid traditions, the false promises and profits are given to the weak, dying and poor. Unruly ideas dedicated by most to remove the last onuses of gold from the pockets of the most desperate. It sickened him mostly. It was all a trick, devised by many for control and greed and the most elaborate joke of them all had been played on an old blind man who welcomed a non-existing spectre to take him away.

Sebastian swayed both of his arms again but stayed in his position in case he fell into a stream or unseen mound that would do damage to him. He now was unaware of what to do, he could not go forwards without the guidance of the wooden staff but the silent object would not move. All around him was motionless until a breeze moved his person slightly. in front of him, some distance away was a tree of some considerable size. It stood tall against the clouded sky that hung over it and seemed to be the only structure to tower over Sebastian. The hard barked trunk of this tree spread out as far as it could, letting bulks of it sprawl out in certain places creating cracks and grooves telling the stories of ages. The roots of the grand timber spread out from its base with each one anchoring the great being to the ground to stop it from tumbling to the earth. Should the being decided to hit the earth it would have been judged that all living creates would have taken fear to their hearts. It stood outright to its grassy surroundings and stretched prominently to the heavens. Branches stemmed from the main trunk, went boundlessly towards all directions around it and found themselves covered in dark green leaves, each abundant in growth. It was magnificent and yet its presence was a complete loss on the old blind man. His darkness still destructed his ability to view the great, old one of the field and instead he was more interested to listen to the wind in the field. It rushed past him, quickly in effect and got stronger with each contact with the juncture of Sebastian's stitches. The old blind man stood fast again and raised himself to the world. He had had enough of the journey had been placed on and now with the freedom of his hands and no direction for him to be taken in, he felt his voice raise from the pits of his soul.

"I want answers?" he bellowed to the heavens above him, "Your sullied practical jokes on me have worn thin, I have but one ally in this world, he is silent but now he has been rendered motionless too, and I know it is by your doing, whoever you are? I have been the point of focus for much hatred in my last few years of life. I have watched my child die, watched my mother die. Has this been for nothing? I have been hindered by my nature, I watched my wife fall away, and I will admit I did nothing to help her. I admit I brought my afflictions on myself. I refused to let others tell me about their positions on matters they could not even see, and for that, I was punished. I cast doubt and saw it for what it was. A fraud. A trick to levy gold from the pockets of the many. I spoke out against those who called me friend once and I spat in their direction. Now I have been dragged miles, miles I say. For what purpose? I have not been informed. I have instead been led on a wild chase across lands. I have had politeness forced onto me by those who in some eyes would be considered barbarians. For reasons unknown, Now whoever you are. You will tell me.

His pain drove his head forward with his last words, throwing spirit in front of him. His shoulders slumped forward and with what small energy the old blind man had, he caught himself before falling to the ground. Defiantly, he refused to fall to his knees and break in front of the instigator of any of his long trailed quest. Dark thoughts clouded his mind. "What if there was no answer?" He was low on all his resolve. What if he had imagined the voices? the staff did not have a will of its own? He could not keep his attention in one place as theories to how he had arrived that this space in all the lands. "Why here?" stress ravaged him as he stood hunched over gathering his strength. He had not considered collapsing where he stood for fear of losing his chance, his one chance to finger out what trick had been played on him. He refused to fall to the ground, he refused. He swung his arms madly again, trying to find the truth that had avoided him. He stretched his finger out far in all directions hoping to feel one answer to end his misery but all he found was his motionless wooden guide, standing silently in the breeze. Sebastian began to give up hope. The sun had started to set without him noticing it being unable to. The fog with its murky aisle gave off a vibrant golden red colour, illuminating the claustrophobia that had been generated by the endless wall of the unknown. Vague strains of warm waves fell on Sebastian's skin, allowing the old man to raise his head to be greeted by the sunlight he had not felt in what seemed to him to be years. He straightens himself up all that he could and breathed in deeply. He counted to three, took another breath, held it and tried to calm down. Maybe this was it. Nothing much to explain, some sort of child's trick that made him walk to the middle of nowhere, someone might have poisoned the food he had eaten, maybe the Confessors were behind this, driving him to the ends of the earth, following him to make sure he continues on all of his journeys to be tormented forever, never to find the peace he desired. Still unknown to him the lands around him turned the colour of gold, the mist around him burned, creating a warm glow of colours. Reds, yellows, oranges and ochre graced the skin of the old man, turning it from its translucent covering of his veins to an immediate shining clothe. His face felt the warmth even more, as his aches and pains started to subdue. His wavers drifted from his mind and raised from his body pulling him up as they ascended towards the sky. The tired motions in his breath lessened and he was able to stand tall. The atmosphere around him shifted and with more complete standing in his mind, old Sebastian heard a voice in his darkness. "Sebastian" the voice rang out in his mind with the heavenly tones played on stringed instruments, unlike the one played by Edward of the Confessors. It soothed the savage beasts of his heart, the tormenting vermin that cowered in lower parts of his mind and the regenerated the dying roots of his being that failed to flower for some time. He gasped in awe at the majesty of the glorious encounter the voice had laid to him. His speech slowed into this through and could not escape his mouth to ask the questions of who is there, instead he remained silent with only the notes of the choir chorus that seemed to accompany this voice. He beckoned in its favour waiting on its next notes and after a while of basing in what he could not explain at these moments, the voice decided to dress him again. "Come forward, gentle Sebastian. Our own selves have been held on your arrival since we arranged for you to arrive. Please step forward, there are only a few paces to go." The old blind man stood opened mouthed at where he thought the feminine voice was coming from. Static for a few seconds as the voice seemed to shake away his aches and even start to implant a feeling of youth in his being, he placed one foot in front of himself, ventured his arm out to his side and placed it on his former wooden guide. It was lighter than it had been, humble in its own way. Sebastian felt about it, he was not going to leave something that had taken him all this way. It too would experience his achievement to make it this far. His old friend had brought him to this spot, but it too was feeling the effects of time and distance. Sebastian ran a hand up the staff for a better grip and notices part of the once smooth crook started to form small cracks in it, where the parts had opened dust fell towards the ground and slight amounts of sand dithered away as it was lifted from its resting area. His old wooden friend had seemed to reach the later stages of his life. Once its main goal had been achieved it was to return to what it was made out of, to begin with. Sebastian held the staff by his side and walked forwards, "My friend, you have carried me this far, I shall help you to come closer." he said with a subtle motion as for no one who might be around to hear him. He walked forwards towards the tree pulling the husk that was he was founded by his skeleton. He stepped forwards closer and closer until the warmth covered his fall front facing half and he let his robe hang less on himself to shed the extra heat he had taken on.

His steps left him closer and closer to the great, stoic tree that dominated the landscape around him, it was the only real thing to stand out and now was a become to all who could see its magnificence, unfortunately, no eyes in the area had the ability to gaze on it for what brilliance it was. Sebastian stepped closer and closer and close to his destination but unable to realise the roots his feet had almost come in contact with, rather than let him fall and cause himself some ruin on him the glorious voice spoke out with its golden tones and stopped him in his tracks. "That's far enough Sebastian," the voice levying him to a halt and allowing the blind man to ease his journey. "Our eyes envisaged you to arrive here, we have waited on you to arrive, to grace this world with his strength, to continue and now you are here". Sebastian stood, taking in all that he could, waiting on himself to recover enough to understand or at least, ask questions to whose presents he resided in. Finally, he spoke, "Who are you?" it was all he could muster from his being. "We are the gods, we have no name but we have always been here. Growing with the world, as life had graced the earth, we had been with it." Sebastian marvelled at the voice which now was echoed with the sounds of other voices, male and female around it as the chorus spoke. They entwined throughout each other, rapping their golden tones over one another on top of one prominent voice of a woman and backed by singing sprites that Sebastian could only imagine. The tree's leaves shined glistening flecks of light from their points, nurturing the ground below them. "We have been groaning for the one such as you," the voice said, "one who is willing to roam the paths too dangerous for many to navigate through lands scattered with those in need of help and too ke..." "What of the other gods?" Sebastian asked, his voice had uttered words that interrupted the heavenly main voice, stopping it from continuing. "What other gods?" the voice replied with echoes covering it with glory from warmed notes. "The gods of the water, the earth, Ximis, Goddess of the Beginning, those ones?" he spoke out, if one god was here in front of him, existing, then maybe the others were real, he could find answers. "There is only us" The voice replied "there are no others but us, we arouse some time ago, we had watched you all grow, humans, animals, we watched you evolve and how you came to be." These words puzzled Sebastian, these where the only gods around and yet he had never heard of them, no stories, no icons, not a drawn figure in a cave or an altar dedicated to them.

"We watched you all unable to interact. We waited, let the lands grow, the mountains form, allowed the sky to bring the rains and allowed you all to grow. Then the stories were told, the stories gathered followings, the followers built temples, stories became doctrines, worshipped the legends and punished those who did not adhere to them. Wars engorged the lands, people were put to death for and by the ones they loved. Then came the shysters, false profits who spread more lies on the land to acquire more funds and power for themselves. Soon the lands had hundreds of thousands of gods that had very come to being."

Sebastian listened with one ear stuck out towards where he believed the voices were coming from. He listened to their tales with fated senses and held his breath to stop from interrupting. The voices began again.

"After an age, we began to grow ourselves. We amassed together and formed this great oak, allowed it to gather its strength to be the biggest, from all the lands. We spawned the foreground this stop to hide ourselves from prying eyes until we were ready, we created desserts to the south, allowed sand dunes to cover towns, increased the rains and made rivers burst to wipe away towns. We treated slight objects from things we found in the air, we could not create the living but we could affect the objects with no life, make wood from dust. So we gathered our strength and we waited, we waited until we found you. We needed one such as yourself, one who had shaken off the corruption of all those other fake deities that clouded men's minds. One who had experience and understanding to roam the earth. We needed you, the blind man, whose words could not be ignored by many, who was not afraid to stand and shout our message to the ears of all on this world. We are now in need of followers and we found you to deliver the sermons."

Sebastian stood in front of the gathering of gods, turned his ears closer to the voices that he could hear the meanings of their truths. It seemed to him that the request they seemed to be building up to would continue his journeys. The old blind man was far from in need of another journey, instead, his wants could have lead him more towards laying under the tree and forever finding peace while surviving off the lands around the area. Tending to what needed to be, locally. Parts of the wooden staff in his hand dissolved with a firm grasp and Sebastian in turn relaxed his grip on his former animated guide. He stood in the shadow of the great tree while the sounds of the heavenly voices filled his ears with their exaltations. He became slightly agitated as the speeches went on, and aches graced a position inside his mind, leading to throbbing moments in his dark relief and with such little want to account for their information, he raised his voice to the plant holding the gods. "What is it that you want of me, I simply have been dragged here by your will, and you seemed to address skill that, if I have been not able to use to the best of my ability. I have seen things in my early life. The messages of gods, and what people understand and take to heart from them. I have seen a lot of suffering contributed to them and now what?" he raised his arms to as high as he could to gesture his contempt with the gods, letting his hands stretch to as far as they could and allowing the staff to rest on his person without it falling to dust. "We are in need of you to convince others." The voice replied "The humans of this earth, that we are the true gods. To spread the spirit to the winds, the earth, the water and life itself, so all can understand and live in peace." Sebastian laughed at their reply, he took on a mocking tone with the gods. "You wish for me to be like Osyrus? He was kept in the mouth of a leviathan for weeks until his destination, is that my destiny on this repeating journey, after journey, and if no one is converted? what then? Do you turn them to sand, stone, wood? Just like the other fictional gods, worship or punishment awaits you." The voice paused a few moments, the new preacher of their divine wisdom had mocked their intension and challenged them in a way that had not before. "You can convince them" the voice spoke out, raining its words on the lands with warming rays of light. "You are the preacher, you will convince all to rise up and look into the light." Sebastian smiled mockery on his new divine commander. He had gathered his strength together with his anger that he had been carrying around with him for years. "Why would I? What is in it for me? What can you do almighty spectre of the world? Will you regrow my eyes in my skull? Give me the gift of sight so I can cast vision on those who will be washed clean with your holy words?" The voice replied, "We cannot undo what has already been set in motion. Your affliction cannot be healed. We cannot create or interact with the organs of the living" The words left old Sebastian cold, he stood in front of the most powerful beings he had ever met and they could not undo the horrors that had been done to him.

"Then what for? Hubris? The good feeling of will and the will of good feeling? I will be a blight, that is all. Who could bother to listen to me? I could not convince a girl to not drown herself. An event that in your divine comedy you sat and watched. Unnamed gods of this great oak tree, I could not convince a woman who believed she had no choice but to end her future, in more ways than one. I could not change her mind, and if you could stop her ways, why would you let it happen in the first place? Why allow families to cast out their children, for them to allow themselves to carry out acts that could have been avoided? Why allow villages to hang those who cannot change their physical ideals? Why allow the greedy to butcher the meek or allow entire entities to go to war and fight them in the names of false gods? If you are only the suggestion in the wind, what good are you? You wish for followers, herding them with an amount of empty promises and hushed tones that will lead to misunderstandings, and what offerings to you should the people have? Days, weeks months of fasting? Festivals? their feed from the crops they have grown, to be left temple altars built by the bloody hands of slaves? All that I had to witness, just to spread the words of another group of gods with another set of plans."

Silence graced the winds, as the last of old Sebastian's hair stood while being moved by the breeze. He had challenged the very being of faith in the dismal streets near the bazaar, where he begged for food. He had lost his eyes because of it and now he stood defiant against it. No heavenly voices graced his ears now, nor did the voice try to return answers to his question but instead he felt the pain intensify in his joints, scars and open wounds trying to heal. His words cut into the divine beings and should he have come across a way to hack at the wooden oak, crashing it to the ground and cleaving it from the earth. Instead of bowing in courteous obedience, he stood as tall as he could, with his arms hanging by his sides. "If the chance should have arrived that would get my sight back, I would rather not." He replied, shouting at the immortal spirits. "Never will I be in your debt." The words of the tired old blind man scorched the earth around him, It left a bigger sullenness in its wake. No reply came, for the few moments, he stood defiant against the voices commanding him to continue his journeys across the earth. The old man breathed heavy, he tried to catch what little of his breath he had and coughed which moved his lungs. He waited on an answer of disappointment or rage from the deities that he believed towered above him, he waited for lightning to strike him or the ground to open up and crush him beneath the soil, surrounding him forever but nothing happened. He coughed again, blood-filled his mouth slightly and he wiped his lip. "Is that your answer?" a more masculine voice replied bringing back the golden glow slightly. Then was echoed by a heavenly female voice and the chorus after that. The voice had changed to a more serious tone, given deep rumblings and force that shocked the grounds slightly. "Of course that is my answer" the old blind man replied his fist clenched, boiling the anger inside himself. "Gods, what in all their judgement can they do. You have admitted that all the other gods are false, false prophets with egos to tend to. My preaching will not persuade people, families, hordes of misguided souls to give up the faith that they have dedicated their lives to. They will see through the false threats that you have decreed on to me, If it was up to me, all words that utter the same pearls of wisdom that you have used to fabricate your treasures would be banished from this earth. You, You of all allow children to suffer, men to commit devastating acts and women to bear witness to fanciful truths. I would rather you be forgotten than spread your legend across the world and may you fade into the unknown, never to be heard of again." The old blind man spat blood onto the grassy centre below him, The throbbing in his head had grown greater than it had before, the pain in his wounds took over his physical being and he felt a heavy wait on his chest. Not even the presence of the unnamed gods that lead him through the lands could stop the feeling under his skin from turning to fire. With his last act of defiance, Sebastian turned from where he was facing the voices that graced him, placed his feet down a few steps, striding away from the great oak and then fell forward. With his last act of rebellion, his heart stopped while having his back turned on the gods that had decreed him the pilgrimage and died before hitting the ground, dropping his wooden guide in the process. He fell front first to the ground stretching his withered frame out as the grass received his lifeless husk. His wired skeleton covered by the rags he had draped around himself flittered in the breeze while parts of his lifeless effort seeped into the world below him. A great wake opened over the reposed body of the dead old man with a hum vibrating over his remains with no success in removing what he had left behind, the stain of defiance at the foot of the grand old oak tree. Old Sebastian's faces settled in the grass, dried by the ever-shining light of the gods, his body remained still as the intense shine from the gods faded back into the grey moody mist that again clouded the lands. The heavens opened and it started to rain slowly. His wooden staff fell apart into dust and ash. With a small sprite of wind, it separated into the gale and partly covered the body of its former possessor and then leaving him forever with his back to the gods.

The End

Printed in Great Britain
by Amazon